Water-blue Eyes

Domingo Villar was born in 1971 and lives in Madrid. He is a radio food critic, a frequent contributor to various periodicals and has also written scripts for film and television. *Water-blue Eyes* won both the Brigada 21 Prize for best first crime novel, as well as the Sintagma Prize. Domingo Villar is currently working on the second instalment in the series featuring Inspector Caldas.

Martin Schifino is a freelance writer and translator. He regularly contributes essays and reviews to *The Times Literary Supplement*, *Revista de Libros* and *Revista Otra Parte*. He is co-translator of José Luis de Juan's *This Breathing World* and Eugenio Fuentes's *Blood of the Angels.* He lives in London.

DOMINGO VILLAR

Water-blue Eyes

Translated from the Spanish by Martin Schifino

Arcadia Books Ltd
15–16 Nassau Street
London W1W 7AB

www.arcadiabooks.co.uk

First published in the United Kingdom by Arcadia Books 2008
This B format edition published 2009

Originally published by Ediciones Siruela as *Ojos de Agua* 2006
Copyright © Domingo Villar 2006

This English translation from the Spanish
Copyright © Martin Schifino 2008

Domingo Villar has asserted his moral right to be identified as the author of this work in
accordance with the Copyright, Designs and Patents Act, 1988.

A catalogue record for this book is available from the British Library.

ISBN 978-1-906413-25-5

Designed and typeset in Minion by Discript Limited, London WC2N 4BN
Printed in Finland by WS Bookwell

Arcadia Books Ltd acknowledges the financial support of la Dirección General del Libro,
Archivos Bibliotecas del Ministerio de Educación, Cultura y Deporte de España.

Arcadia Books supports English PEN, the fellowship of writers who work together to
promote literature and its understanding. English PEN upholds writers' freedoms in
Britain and around the world, challenging political and cultural limits on free expression.
To find out more, visit www.englishpen.org, or contact
English PEN, 6–8 Amwell Street, London EC1R 1UQ.

Arcadia Books distributors are as follows:

in the UK and elsewhere in Europe:
Turnaround Publishers Services
Unit 3, Olympia Trading Estate
Coburg Road
London N22 6TZ

in the USA and Canada:
Independent Publishers Group
814 N. Franklin Street
Chicago, IL 60610

in Australia:
Tower Books
PO Box 213
Brookvale, NSW 2100

in New Zealand:
Addenda
Box 78224
Grey Lynn
Auckland

in South Africa:
Quartet Sales and Marketing
PO Box 1218
Northcliffe
Johannesburg 2115

Arcadia Books is the *Sunday Times* Small Publisher of the Year

To Beatriz, my love, whose eyes bring me closer to the sea.

Dark

The line of lights on the coast, the glimmer of the city, the white spray where the waves broke... It made no difference that it was dark and the rain was lashing against the windows. Whoever was visiting his flat for the first time invariably mentioned the view, as if compelled.

Luis Reigosa picked a CD from the shelf, put it on the hi-fi and poured the drinks into wide glasses, the rims of which he'd previously rubbed with lemon peel. He couldn't have known they'd be the last he'd ever pour.

They listened to the roar of the wind as they went into the bedroom with their arms around each other. From the living room, Billie Holliday reached out to them with 'The man I love':

> *Some day he'll come along*
> *The man I love*
> *And he'll be big and strong*
> *The man I love*

1

Tuning

'City police three, Leo nil.'

Leo Caldas put down his uncomfortable headphones, lit up a cigarette and looked out of the window.

Some children were chasing pigeons in the garden, under the attentive gazes both of their mothers, who were chatting in a circle, and of the birds waiting for them to get close before taking flight.

He put his headphones back on when a call came in – a woman wanting to lodge a complaint against the pub beneath her house. The noise, she said, sometimes kept her up until dawn. She complained about the shouting, the music, the beeps of the horns, the parallel parking, the drunken singing, the brawls, the walls sprayed with urine, and the broken glass strewn on the pavement – which constituted a hazard for her child.

Caldas let her get it off her chest, knowing he'd be unable to offer anything but comforting words. That kind of thing was not within the competence of his department, but of the city police.

'I'll send a memo to the city police asking them to gauge the decibels and to make sure closing times are being observed,' he said, writing the address of the pub in his notebook.

He wrote underneath: 'City police four, Leo nil.'

↬

The theme tune of the show played out until Rebeca placed another sign scribbled with black letters against the glass. Leo Caldas took a quick drag on his cigarette and balanced it on the edge of the ashtray.

'Good afternoon, Angel,' Santiago Losada, the presenter,

2

greeted the listener who was waiting on the other end of the line.

'Let us welcome pain if it is cause for repentance,' the man said, enunciating each word clearly.

'Sorry?' the presenter replied, as surprised as Caldas at the strange statement.

'Let us welcome pain if it is cause for repentance,' the man repeated, in the same slow voice as before.

'Excuse me, Angel. You're live on *Patrol on the Air*,' Losada reminded him. 'Do you have any questions for Inspector Caldas?'

The man hung up, leaving the presenter without a reply and cursing under his breath.

'People love to hear themselves on the radio,' apologised Losada, as the ads came on.

Leo Caldas smiled and thought that Losada deserved to be cut down to size every now and again.

'Some more than others,' he muttered.

～

On another call, an elderly man living on the outskirts of the city complained that, at a set of traffic lights near his house, the green light didn't stay on long enough for him to walk across the road.

Leo took down the location of the traffic lights in his notebook. He would let the city police know.

'Five-nil, without counting the crazy guy's call.'

～

The inspector's mobile phone was on silent, but on the table its screen lit up, warning him that he had some missed calls.

He saw there were three, all from his subordinate Estévez, and decided not to respond to them. He was tired and didn't want to drag out the day more than strictly necessary. They'd meet later at the police station, or, with a little luck, the following morning.

He took a long drag to finish his cigarette, stubbed it out into an ashtray and popped his headphones back on to listen to Eva, who told him that certain supernatural apparitions, indeed abominable spectres, unfailingly visited her house every night.

Leo wondered whether Losada should contemplate creating a segment called *Madness on the Air* to accommodate all the visionaries who phoned in so often. When the presenter underlined the name and number of the woman in his diary, he thought Losada just might.

⌒

A few calls later, programme number 108 of *Patrol on the Air* came to an end. Leo Caldas read the final score in his black-covered notebook: 'City police nine, crazies two, Leo nil.'

Ambiguity

The inspector walked into the police station and proceeded down the aisle between two rows of desks. He had often felt, striding between the lined-up computers, that he was in a newsroom rather than in a police station.

Estévez stood up when he saw him appear, and lugged his six-foot-five bulk right behind him.

Caldas opened the frosted-glass door of his office and took a look at the papers stacked on his table. He prided himself on being able to locate anything among the apparent chaos of jottings and documents, though he knew this to be only a half-truth. He slumped into his black leather chair, exhausted after a long day's work, and sighed; he barely knew where to begin.

Rafael Estévez burst in, adding to his worries.

'Inspector, Superintendent Soto called. He wants us to go to this address,' he said, waving a piece of paper. 'Some officers are already there.'

'Between you and the superintendent I can barely sit down for a minute. Do we know what happened at all?'

'No. I told him you were at the radio station with that *Patrol on the Air* idiot, and I offered to come over myself, but he wanted me to wait for you.'

'Let me see.'

Caldas read the address, crumpled the piece of paper and left it on the desk.

'Shit,' he muttered, closing his eyes and leaning back in his chair.

'Are we not going, chief?'

Leo Caldas clicked his tongue.

'Give me a minute, will you?'

'Of course,' replied Estévez, who was still a bit unfamiliar with his superior's manners.

↬

Rafael Estévez had only been in Galicia for a few months. A rumour at the station had it that his transfer had been a punishment administered in his native Zaragoza. The officer had accepted his job in the town of Vigo without any visible displeasure, but he was finding it difficult to adjust to some things here. One was the unpredictable, ever-changing nature of the weather; another the steepness of the streets. The third was ambiguity. To Rafael Estévez's stern Aragonese mind, things were this way or that, got done or didn't, so it was only with considerable effort that he managed to decipher the ambiguous expressions of his new fellow citizens.

↬

He had first come into contact with the local ways three days after arriving, when Superintendent Soto asked him to take a statement from a teenager who had been caught selling marijuana to his schoolmates.

'Name?' Estévez had asked, trying to do it as quickly as possible.

'My name?' asked the boy.

'Yes, lad, I wouldn't be asking for mine, would I?'

'You wouldn't,' the young dealer conceded.

'So tell me your name.'

'Francisco.'

Officer Estévez typed the boy's name.

'Francisco. And then?'

'And then nothing.'

'Haven't you got a surname?'

'Oh, Martín Fabeiro, Franciso Martín Fabeiro.'

Rafael Estévez, sitting in front of his computer, entered the surname and moved the cursor to the next blank on the statement form.

'Address.'

'My address?'

Rafael Estévez looked up. 'Do you think I'd be asking for mine? You don't think this is a game of charades, do you?'

'No, sir.'

'Well then, tell me your address.'

Estévez paused, waiting for the boy's answer, but the question seemed to have thrown him into deep thought.

'Would that be where I normally live?' he said eventually.

'Do you actually sell the pot or smoke it? Of course that would be where you normally live. We need to be able to contact you.'

'The thing is, it depends.'

'How do you mean, it depends? You must have a house like everyone else. Unless you live in the streets, like a cat.'

'No, no sir. I live with my parents.'

'Tell me your address, then,' roared Estévez.

'My parents' address?'

'Look, matey, let's be clear – I'm the one who asks the questions here. Do you understand?'

'Yes, sir.'

'Well, now you understand, you're going to tell me where the fuck you and your family live, do you understand me?' he warned him, visibly put out.

The boy gazed at him, apparently without comprehending why this enormous police officer was getting so worked up.

'I said, do you understand me?' pressed Estévez.

'Yes, sir,' the boy mumbled.

'Well, let's get this over with. I haven't got all morning. Now, where the fuck do you live? And please tell me the address where you *normally* live, not that of the brothel where you father drops by on pay day.'

After another pause, the boy dared to say:

'Do you want the address in town or in the village?'

'Now...' said Estévez, struggling to control himself.

'You see,' the boy hastened to add, 'we're here in the city from Monday to Friday, but at weekends we load the car and go to our village. I can give you either address.'

The boy finished the explanation and awaited new instructions. Estévez looked at him without even blinking.

'Sir?'

The officer pushed the computer aside and lifted the boy half a metre clean off the floor by the lapels. He then grabbed his regulation gun and pointed it at the horrified kid's mouth.

'Do you see this gun? Do you see it, you pathetic clown?'

The boy, his feet hanging in the air and the barrel barely a centimetre from his mouth, nodded in alarm.

'If you don't fucking tell me where you live I'll knock out all your teeth with it and shove them one by one up your arse. Is that clear?'

The superintendent, who was observing from behind a two-way mirror how the newcomer deported himself during interrogations, walked in at that moment and stopped him carrying out his threat. However, he couldn't prevent the episode from triggering all sorts of conjectures about Estévez's fiery personality at the station, or gossip from spreading on the subject of why he had been transferred to Vigo.

To keep the impetuous officer under close surveillance, Soto had entrusted him to Inspector Leo Caldas. And yet Estévez, in spite of the inspector's calm influence, had remained in a constant state of alert. There was something inside him that brushed against the Galician people's inability to call a spade a spade. He saw this attitude as bordering on a compulsion, and refused to believe it might be a mere local trait.

⌐

Leo Caldas read the address on the piece of paper again: Duplex 17/18, North Wing, Toralla Towers.

'Let's go over before it gets dark,' he said, standing up. 'You're going to enjoy the ride.'

Artist

Rafael Estévez got in the car whistling a tune he'd had in his head for several weeks. Leo Caldas sat back in his seat, rolled down the window a crack and closed his eyes.

'I've got to go down to the beach, right, inspector?' the officer asked. His knowledge of the complex local geography was improving, but he still didn't feel entirely at ease among the dense traffic of the city.

Caldas opened his eyes to show him the way.

'Yes, it's the island opposite Canido harbour, which is the first one right after the beaches. You can't miss it.'

'Oh, the island with the high-rise. I know where that is.'

'Let's go then,' replied the inspector, closing his eyes again.

Along the boulevard on the coast, they passed a modern fishing harbour on their right, which had been reclaimed from the sea by filling a narrow cove. Several boats were returning to their moorings with hundreds of seagulls hovering above them in search of a sardine for dinner.

On the left, on the side facing the waterfront, they left behind the old Berbés harbour, where all the seafaring activities of the city had started at the end of the nineteenth century. Its granite arcades, under which the fish had been unloaded in former times, had retreated from the coast as a consequence of the constant expansion of the docks.

The tide was low, and the strong smell of the sea wafted in through the window. Rafael Estévez liked this smell; it was almost new to him. He looked at the landscape, the intricate relief of fjord-like inlets known as *rías,* that had seduced him from the moment he'd seen it. The sea he'd always been familiar with, since the summer holidays of his childhood, was the Mediterranean, which extended as far as the eye could see. In Galicia, however, swaths of green land gave way here and there to *rías* of varying colours, shielded from the pounding of the Atlantic by streamlined, white-sand islands.

Following the boulevard, they went past the shipyards where the armatures of future boats were in view, and then drove into the ring road – a misnomer, since it wasn't a ring at all – until they reached the first beaches. After several rainy days, crowds of people had returned to Samil beach on this mild afternoon, and along its stone promenade joggers, dogs and bicycles went past each other once again. Over the sea, the sky had taken on a reddish colour that heralded nightfall.

At the local sports centre, two teams of children were having a football match. They shouted to each other as they chased the ball, and their airborne voices were audible through the barely opened window. The car rounded the fence of the site and lunged into a sharp bend in the road, near the mouth of the Lagares River. The speed pushed Caldas over to the driver's seat. He opened his eyes, readjusted himself, and watched the children for a few moments. At the next bend, as the orange team was nearing the blue team's goal area, the inspector lost sight of them. Then the centrifugal force threw him against the door of the car.

'For God's sake, Rafael!'

'What's up, inspector?'

'Why can't you drive like a normal person?'

Rafael slowed down. A few seconds later they heard the high-pitched ring of Caldas's mobile.

'That's yours, boss,' said Estévez, when he considered it had rung enough times.

Caldas read the superintendent's name on the screen and answered.

'Leo, did you get the message?' Superintendent Soto seemed as impatient as ever.

'We're on our way,' he confirmed.

'Is Estévez with you?'

'Yes,' ratified Caldas. 'Shouldn't he have come?'

'He shouldn't have been born,' replied Soto and rang off.

They continued along the winding road that skirted the coast. After leaving several built-up areas behind they reached Vao beach. The island came into view right across from it.

Toralla was a small island. There were only a few mansions, beaches and tracts of wilderness on barely twenty hectares opposite the most exclusive residential area of the bay. But something unusual stood out in this small paradise, a twenty-floor high-rise that, at the height of urban brutalism, had been built with no regard for the harmony that the island had preserved until then. Caldas had always thought that if it had been constructed five centuries before, it would have been enough to scare Frances Drake away and send him and his buccaneers back to England.

They left the main road and headed for the access bridge. Estévez stopped the car where it jutted out.

'Do we have to drive across, inspector?'

'Unless you'd rather swim,' replied Caldas, without opening his eyes.

Rafael Estévez, muttering to himself, drove along the two hundred metres of the bridge. To the west, the golden light shimmered on the sea, making it difficult to look at it face on. But to the east one could clearly see the shore, lit by a sun that was almost level with the water.

They left behind the metal staircases descending on to the beach, which was the larger of the two in Toralla. The rocks of the breakwaters, now exposed by the low tide, were covered in green moss.

A barrier and a sentry box controlled access to the island.

'Isn't this open to the public, inspector?'

'Only so far,' replied Caldas.

A security guard came out of the booth with a notepad in his hand, and asked them where they were going. As soon as

Estévez showed his badge, he lifted the barrier and let them through.

The car cleared the surveillance post and proceeded along a narrow road, passing on one side a long row of cottages and on the other a forest of pine trees, whose smell blended perfectly with the smell of the surrounding sea. Where the road forked, they took the right. They skirted the woods until the enormous high-rise appeared before them, making Estévez whistle in admiration.

'Some skyscraper, inspector. It didn't look so high from far off.'

'I hope its foundations are good,' muttered Leo Caldas, who had the conviction that no place was better for setting one's foot than firm ground.

Since most of the flats in that marvel of bad taste were occupied only during the summer, the car park was nearly empty. Caldas identified the van of the inspection unit among the few parked cars. It must be quite serious if they were still there. On getting out of the car, Estévez took a closer look at the tower. He had to tilt his head back to see it whole. He whistled again and followed his boss to the lobby of the building.

There were twenty floors and three wings: north, south and east. Leo Caldas reckoned there must be about ten flats per floor, six hundred of them in total. It must have been too good a real estate deal to deny it planning permission, even if the result was an eyesore.

He reread his piece of paper: 'Duplex 17/18, north wing.'

They followed a sign and entered the lift. Caldas pressed 17. Once out, the inspector went briskly up a short flight of stairs. Estévez followed suit, his footsteps resounding down the hall.

The door was marked out by a police tape blocking the way. Leo Caldas peeled it off from one side and opened the door. Estévez went in behind his boss, not before fixing the crime scene tape back in place.

They came into a large room, the front wall of which was taken up by an enormous curtainless window. The iridescent light of the sunset flooded it with reddish colours. It commanded a superb view, this window: the Cíes Islands right in front; one of the shores of the main *ría* on the left; and, on the right, the Morrazo Peninsula, which jutted out into the sea like a stone gargoyle. Rafael Estévez immediately approached the window the better to appreciate that vista. Caldas did not.

The living room had two sofas and a glass coffee table. Facing the sofas was a state-of-the-art hi-fi instead of a TV. Caldas realised the several small metal boxes scattered about the corners of the room were loudspeakers. A bookshelf packed with CDs took up the back wall.

Adorned with a basket of dry flowers on its centre, and surrounded by four high-backed chairs, the dining table was as far as possible from the window. Across from the shelves hung two engravings. One represented a vase painted with love scenes, the other the frieze of a classical edifice. Beside them, hanging on the same wall, were six saxophones.

Clara Barcia, one of the forensic officers, was in the living room, dusting a couple of glasses for fingerprints.

'Hi, Clara,' Caldas said, as he approached.

'Good afternoon, inspector,' she replied, straightening her back. 'I'm nearly done with the prints.'

'Don't get up, please,' said Caldas, matching his words with a gesture, and taking a look around. 'What have we got here?'

'Murder, inspector. Pretty nasty.'

Caldas nodded, then said:

'And how's your work going?'

'I've collected quite a few samples,' she said, pointing to some small evidence bags she'd lined up against the wall, 'but you never know.'

'Are you on your own?'

'No, initially all four of us came down, but for a while it's been only Doctor Barrio and me. He's downstairs in the bed-room. Over here.'

Clara Barcia put the glass she was examining on the table, stood up and showed them the way down the spiral staircase.

'Are you not coming down, officer?' she asked Estévez through the wooden steps of the staircase.

Caldas turned round and saw his subordinate at the living room window taking in the view. He was surprised to find that this implacable officer, who was capable of softening up the toughest thugs, was showing as much appreciation of the landscape as an artist would.

Estévez took three agile leaps down the stairs and placed himself behind the inspector. Barcia handed a pair of latex gloves to each of them.

'Where's the corpse?' asked Caldas.

'In here, on the bed,' Barcia replied, opening the door to the only bedroom in the flat.

Rafael Estévez, struggling to ease his huge hands into the gloves, opened his mouth for the first time since he'd come in.

'Fucking hell!'

Find

The man's horror-stricken face was a clear indication of the pain he had gone through. His hands were tied to the headboard of the bed with a piece of white cloth, and his naked body was contorted into an unnatural posture. A sheet covered him from the waist down to his feet.

Leo Caldas frowned in a reflex action, shutting his nostrils to keep at bay the foetid waft of decaying flesh. His face relaxed a moment later, as he realised the corpse was too recent to give off the smell of death.

Guzmán Barrio, the forensic doctor examining the corpse, turned round when he heard them walk into the room.

'I had to start without you, Leo,' he said, looking at a watch one could barely make out through his glove.

'I'm sorry, Guzmán. They kept me at the station until the last possible moment. Do you know Rafael Estévez?' asked Caldas, turning towards his subordinate.

'We've seen each other at the station,' the doctor confirmed.

'How's the examination going?' asked Estévez.

'Oh, it's going.'

'I see,' said Estévez. Then he added to himself. 'Why is everyone always so precise round here?'

Leo Caldas approached the bed and inspected the dead man's hands, tightly tied to the headboard. They were big but delicate, and due to the lack of blood they'd taken on a bluish shade that contrasted with his pale arms. From the deep marks round his wrists it could be deduced that he had struggled to free himself until pretty much his last breath.

'Do we know who he is?' he asked.

It was Clara Barcia who answered.

'Luis Reigosa, thirty-four years old. A native of Breu. He was a professional musician, a saxophonist. Concerts, lessons, and so on... He lived alone, and had been renting this flat for a couple of years.'

Caldas experienced a familiar unease as he heard the concise biographical details about the man.

⌒

Until he joined the police force, the only dead body Leo Caldas had seen from up close was that of his mother lying in her coffin. He hadn't even asked to see her, but had agreed to it when someone mentioned it was the last chance to say goodbye. Suddenly he was lifted off the ground, and he found himself in someone's arms, as if levitating, peering over that dark wooden box in which the inert body of his mother lay wrapped in a shroud. In a state of confusion, he had looked at a face seemingly covered with a strange coat of wax, and in those brief seconds that he remembered as lasting an eternity, a few of his tears had splattered on the glass sealing the coffin. His mother's sunken eyes were closed, and her pale lips were barely distinguishable from the rest of her face, a colour that was in sharp contrast to the lipstick she had applied even until her last days.

For years that indelible waxen image had visited his dreams. And he had often remembered his father at the wake, sitting in a corner, his face transfigured with pain yet not shedding one tear.

At the police academy some time later, when he was still a recruit, he'd often been warned he was bound to find himself faced with a violent death. Caldas had felt scared and expectant of that future personal encounter, as well as uncertain of what his reaction might be.

He had soon found out, on one of his first nights on duty, when he and his partner were called to a park where a homeless man had been stabbed to death. Not without surprise, he discovered that seeing the unknown man's body didn't shock him at all. He didn't even hesitate to approach it. And from that first time, dead bodies were to Leo Caldas little more than lost property. When he was at a crime scene, whether a body was still warm or in a state of decay, he effortlessly detached himself from the fact that the remains had once breathed life. He concentrated on gathering the evidence that might help solve the causes of death, on collecting the disparate pieces of the puzzle that he must put together.

And yet, as soon as he learned the identities of the deceased he felt an inner shudder; for once he knew their names or, however sketchily, certain aspects of their lives, it was as if the actual human beings arrived on the scene of the criminal investigation.

↩

'Did you say he lived alone?' asked Caldas, who could tell by the state of the body that he hadn't been dead for long.

Officer Barcia nodded.

'Who informed us of the death?' he asked, surprised that the corpse had been found so quickly.

'It was the security guard on the bridge,' replied Clara Barcia, 'though the body was actually found by the cleaner. She comes in twice a week. Apparently the poor woman turned up at the sentry box in a state of shock after seeing the body. She had to be sedated, so we'll have to wait till tomorrow to speak to her. Officer Ferro wrote it all down. He must be at the station writing up the report.'

Caldas nodded. He was sorry to be late, even more so since the reason was *Patrol on the Air*.

'When do you reckon he was killed?' asked the inspector.

'Last night,' replied Barrio. 'From the body temperature I'd say between seven and twelve last night. But I'm afraid I can't be more specific until we do the post-mortem.'

'If you don't need me here, I'll go back to work,' said Clara.

She left the room and disappeared up the spiral staircase. Leo remained still in front of the dead man. He couldn't stop looking at his open eyes. They were of a very light blue and seemed to be staring at him in horror.

'Do we know how he died?' asked Rafael Estévez, turning to the doctor.

'Reigosa?'

'No, Lady Di,' said Rafael, cutting him short.

'Don't mind him, Guzmán, Rafael is always this polite,' Leo Caldas put in. 'In any case, do we know the cause of death?'

'Not the exact cause, but I can assure you this had a lot to do with it,' he replied, removing the sheet that so far covered the dead man's abdomen, 'even if I can't be more precise for now.'

'Holy fuck, what's *that* he's got there?' exclaimed Estévez, cupping his testicles and moving away from the body.

'That's what I was trying to find out when you arrived,' the doctor said. 'I still don't know for sure.'

The body displayed a huge area of bruised skin. The damage started at his stomach and extended down to his legs. On one of them, the unsettling blackness reached down to the knee. The skin was so shrivelled up that Caldas had the impression that he had a tanned hide before him rather than human skin. He'd never seen anything like it. Judging from Doctor Barrio's astonished expression, he hadn't either.

'I'm sorry, doctor, did you say the stiff was called Reigosa?' asked Estévez, approaching once again to take a closer look.

'Apparently so,' the doctor conceded.

'And where's the guy's dick, if you don't mind me asking?'

Barrio placed his tissue forceps on a small protuberance at the centre of the grotesque haematoma.

'What do you think the blackest bit is?'

Estévez pored over the area that the doctor indicated.

'*That?*'

The doctor nodded, and Estévez looked at his superior in disbelief.

'Did you see that, inspector – this guy would need a doctor's forceps even to go and take a leak.'

Leo Caldas came closer the better to inspect the body. The

kinds of bruises he had come across until then gave the impression of tumescence. But if that was a tumescent sex, he didn't want to imagine the regular size of Reigosa's penis. It looked like the empty shell of a barnacle: dark and wrinkled. And one could just make out, as black as all the rest, the saxophonist's testicles. They were the size of raisins, and had the same texture. He turned towards the doctor, as if asking for further information.

'I'm going crazy trying to guess how anyone managed to damage the tissue so badly, but I can't figure it out. I've thought of fire or any other heat source, but then there's no burning on the skin. See?' said the doctor as he moved Reigosa's minute member this way and that. 'It's all leathery, in a very strange way. I haven't found any wounds or blood... I'm beginning to think they poured some kind of abrasive substance on him.'

'The pain must have been excruciating,' said Caldas, visualising the scene Guzmán Barrio had just presented. 'And no one heard anything? Even if only a few people live here at this time of year, someone must have heard the screams.'

Barrio pointed at a piece of tape and a wet white ball placed on the night table beside the bed.

'When we found him, he was gagged with that. They rammed the cotton nearly all the way down his throat, and then sealed his lips with the tape. There's no way anyone would hear you with that in your mouth.'

They fell silent as they looked at the dead saxophonist.

'It must have been harrowing. Have you seen his eyes?' said Doctor Barrio, breaking the silence, as if he were trying to know whether the inspector was as stunned as he.

Leo Caldas nodded and looked again at those eyes that had moved him from the first moment. Seen close-to they made an even greater impact on him. They revealed the pain to which Reigosa had been subjected with such cruelty – a mute torment, as he hadn't even been able to scream. He remembered reading words by Camus to the effect that the

19

human being is born, dies and is not happy. He couldn't know, but he guessed the existence of this man, lying here livid and lifeless, had been like that.

'I've never seen eyes like that. Don't they look unreal?' asked Caldas as he pointed at Reigosa's face.

'They do,' replied Barrio. 'At first I actually thought they were contacts. But they aren't. His eyes really were that colour, water-blue.'

꩜

Reigosa's room was large, clean, filled with the same reddish light as the rest of the flat. On the wall over the bed hung a framed poster, a reproduction of Hopper's *Hotel Room*. Caldas remembered the original painting. He'd seen it with Alba at the Thyssen Museum in Madrid. He'd been dazzled by the loneliness of the woman sitting on the bed, by her serene beauty and sad mien. In front of the poster, Caldas once again had the impression that the painter, in portraying her in that pink nightdress, with her suitcase half packed, had profaned her intimacy. And he wondered whether they, as Hopper had in his own way, were not violating Reigosa's.

The wall opposite the bed was also one big window. It wasn't as big as the one in the living room, but it commanded similar views. Caldas didn't go near it.

On the night table there were two books, one on top of the other. The top one, which had a bookmark inserted among its six hundred-odd pages, was *Lectures on the Philosophy of History*. Caldas picked it up with a gloved hand and read the name of its author on the back cover: 'Georg Wilhelm Friedrich Hegel (Stuttgart, 1770–Berlin, 1831)'.

Estévez approached from behind.

'*Lectures on the Philosophy of History*,' he read. 'You must suffer from insomnia if you can read this kind of stuff in bed without falling asleep. Don't you think, inspector?'

'Perhaps that's exactly what he had it for,' answered Caldas tersely.

The inspector glanced again at the body, still tied to the

bed with his horribly bruised genitals exposed. It was an undignified death for a musician with an interest in philosophy. He put the thick volume on the night table and picked up the other one: *The Terracotta Dog* by Andrea Camilleri.

Nor were these two the only books in the room. On the wall opposite the door there were several packed bookshelves. Caldas remembered his father, who always said you can know a man from what he reads and what he drinks. He was surprised to find almost exclusively crime novels on the musician's shelves: Montalbán, Ellroy, Chandler, Hammett...

'The order of last night's events seems clear.' Guzmán Barrio was thinking out loud, as he carried on examining Reigosa's inert body. 'A few drinks in the living room, then they came down to the bedroom, had sex and, when this guy was at his most trusting, his lover tied him up, gagged him and murdered him. I wonder why they didn't do it in a simpler way. This,' he said, gesturing towards Reigosa's gruesome stomach, 'whatever it was they did, must have been a lot more difficult, more dramatic.'

'You can't really mean he screwed with that?' put in Estévez, pointing with his hand to the dead man's minute penis.

'Rafael, do me a favour, will you, go and see what you can find in the living room,' asked Caldas, pointing him in the direction of the door.

But once Estévez disappeared up the stairs, Caldas turned towards the doctor and asked: 'Guzmán, do you actually think he had intercourse?' He knew this would open the most important line of inquiry.

The doctor shook his head in an ambiguous manner, making a movement that didn't quite mean yes or no.

'I cannot be sure, but on a first examination it seems possible. At least I don't think we should rule it out, in spite of what the member looks like now. In any case, I need to carry out a complete post-mortem before I can confirm it either way. Why don't you drop by tomorrow? Today we can't reject any possibility,' he concluded.

As yet, Guzmán Barrio hadn't found any signs of violence besides the obvious ones in the genital area and the wrists. The doctor ascribed only the former to the murderer. Like Caldas, he believed the chafing round the wrists had been produced by Reigosa in a desperate attempt to free himself.

Guzmán Barrio believed that what they had there was a crime of passion: all the clues pointed that way. There wasn't any disturbance in the room, as is often the case following a fight, and this lent weight to the theory that the dead man had not been forcibly tied up. The inspector thought Reigosa knew the murderer, or at least that the murderer had not aroused any suspicions in him. It seemed logical to assume that he wouldn't have let himself be tied up if he had sensed any danger.

'Will you have anything by morning?' asked Caldas impatiently.

'Can you make it noon?'

The inspector moved closer to the night table and looked at the photograph on it. He prised apart the wooden frame and took the picture out. Reigosa was smiling and fondly holding his saxophone, as if they were a couple of teenage lovers. It was a black-and-white picture, and the dead musician's nearly transparent blue eyes came out in a very light grey.

'Guzmán, I'm taking this with me,' he said, slipping the picture into the inside pocket of his jacket.

Before leaving the downstairs floor, Leo went to take a look at the bathroom. It was all done up in white marble, with expensive-looking taps and a large hydrotherapy bath. The towels, white too, were clean and neatly piled. Thinking it was no small luxury for a jazz-club musician, he left for the living room. If there were any hairs on the floor, a trace of urine in the toilet or any other clue that might help them identify the killer, it would not go unnoticed by the methodical work of forensics.

On the top floor, Estévez was looking out of the window. Clara Barcia had moved on to the carpet in her systematic search for clues. She had turned all the lights on and divided the room into squares marked off with pieces of string. The evidence found in each of them was put into plastic bags and labelled accordingly.

Caldas noticed the glasses on the coffee table. The drinks bore out the theory that Luis Reigosa had been with someone he knew, or at least with someone who hadn't taken him by surprise. He bent down to sniff one of the glasses, and clearly recognised the dry, penetrating smell of gin. He checked the rim to see if there were any lip marks and immediately made out some faint traces of lipstick.

'Have you checked for prints on the bottles?' he asked the forensics officer.

'They are all in the kitchen, inspector,' she replied, nodding.

Leo Caldas looked around. The kitchen was nowhere to be seen.

'It's here,' said Clara Barcia as she stood up. She opened a sliding door that Caldas had believed to be a cupboard, and a tiny kitchen appeared. 'They're called compact kitchens. They're all right if you don't cook much, as they take up little space, clearly.'

Caldas moved towards it, but Clara Barcia stopped him.

'I'm sorry, inspector. There are quite a few prints in there I haven't had time to check yet.'

'Of course,' he said, moving away to allow Clara to close the door. He knew how meticulous she was when it came to inspecting hot spots at a crime scene, so he didn't mind his curiosity being checked by an officer of lower rank. On the contrary, he was glad he could count on Clara Barcia's expertise for this investigation. He valued her powers of observation and her infinite patience in hunting the tiniest pieces of evidence.

The inspector drew near the saxophones hanging on the

wall. The oldest of them was the one Reigosa was holding in the picture he now had in his pocket. Caldas stroked its cold metal hump with the back of his hand, as if offering it his condolences.

In the living room, hundreds of CDs, almost all of jazz, were stacked up on five shelves. The top shelf featured female vocalists, while the three others housed an admirable collection entirely devoted to the saxophone. Among many unknown names, the inspector recognised some he was quite familiar with, such as Sonny Rollins, Lester Young and Charlie Parker. On the bottom shelf were dozens of scores. Leo Caldas picked one at random, which turned out to be *Stella by Starlight* for tenor sax, by Victor Young. He knew the piece, and had it at home in a version by Stan Getz.

Although he couldn't read music, he flicked through the score, poring over the symbols curling on the lines of the stave, and hummed the melody to himself. He remembered with a touch of nostalgia the Sunday afternoons Alba had christened 'of music and letters', during which some of these very musicians had kept them company as Alba and he, dressed only in their pyjamas, read lying on the sofa.

'Have you seen the CDs, chief?' asked Estévez, still standing in front of the window.

Caldas nodded.

'Our friend of the tiny fried penis must have been a bit queer, don't you think?'

'What's that got to do with anything?'

'Don't get me wrong, chief. I'm not bothered who people choose to sleep with. This is a free country.'

'No need to make excuses,' said the inspector, encouraging him to go on.

'But you only need to take a look at all those funny CDs, the paintings right there or the one over the bed to guess this guy was a friend of Dorothy's.'

'Just because of that it doesn't mean ...'

'Just because of that?' repeated Estévez. 'What did you expect, chief, a poster with a young lad in the buff?'

The inspector realised his subordinate had not seen the lipstick traces on the glasses, but he chose to keep silent rather than contradict him, as he saw Officer Barcia casting wary glances at Estévez.

'Drop it, Rafael,' he muttered, sensing that if he let Estévez take this line of reasoning any further, there would be even more gossip about him at the station.

Clara Barcia finished scrutinising one of the squares marked on the carpet and moved on to the next, the nearest one to the hi-fi. When she bent down, she flicked a switch without meaning to, and a warm woman's voice suddenly filled every corner of the room.

> Day in, day out
> That same old voodoo follows me about.

The young officer looked in vain for the switch to stop the music.

'Sorry, so sorry,' she said, blushing a little for her clumsiness.

'You can leave it on, it's fine by me,' replied Caldas, reassuring her that it didn't matter at all.

'What is this?' growled Estévez.

'Billie Holliday,' said the inspector as he walked over to the hi-fi and turned up the volume. Clara smiled and kneeled back down within her square of carpet marked off with pieces of string.

> That same old pounding in my heart,
> Whenever I think of you.
> And baby I think of you.
> Day in and day out.

Estévez went back to the window and looked at the landscape that had allowed him to forget the dead man's genitals for a moment.

'Do you know what I like best about this high-rise, inspector?'

'That you can't see the high-rise from here?' replied Caldas, without coming close to the window.

Estévez remained silent, and Billie Holliday moaned once again.

When there it is, day in, day out.

The Bar

Caldas was walking down the pavement of Príncipe Street, which bore hardly any trace of its earlier hustle and bustle. The shops were now closed, and there was barely anyone about. Most people had abandoned this part of town and, taking advantage of the wonderful May evening, had chosen the boulevard by the sea for their evening stroll.

The inspector was on his way back from the city police station, in the town City Hall, where he had presented the officer on duty with a file containing the catalogue of complaints, addresses and telephone numbers which he had collected at the radio station. He had asked Estévez not to wait for him. He preferred to walk home. He liked the city at night, when he could hear his footsteps rhythmically resounding on the pavement, and when the smell of trees prevailed over the exhaust smoke of cars. Besides, the empty streets were ideal for going over the inspection at the high-rise on Toralla Island. From the moment he'd left Reigosa's place he'd had the nagging feeling that he had missed something. Unable to put his finger on it for now, he followed the bend to the right in Príncipe Street, only ten or twelve steps after its start. He reached a square closed off by a one-storey stone house.

The stone façade had a Galician emigrant drawn on it, one of the many whom poverty had forced into exile, like the ones portrayed by the artist Daniel Alfonso Rodríguez Castelao in his illustrations. Beneath it, there were words once uttered by Castelao himself: 'I'll be back when Galicia is free'. He had died in Buenos Aires.

The door and the two windows were made of wood and painted green. A few cast-iron letters, which had been screwed into the stone, formed a word in a childish handwriting: 'Eligio'.

Leo Caldas pushed the door open.

Since Eligio had taken charge of the bar several decades before, its rustic walls had given shelter to the intellectual cream of the town. The staff of the *Pueblo Gallego* newspaper, which was to be found only a few metres away, had led the way, attracted by the excellent house wines. And, little by little, lawyers, literati, poets, painters and politicians had come to place themselves near the cast-iron stove of the establishment.

Sitting in a corner, Lugrís had drawn medusas, seahorses and ships which seemed sunk in the marble table. And a few of his colleagues, long on talent but short on funds, had left their legacies painted on the walls, thus linking them forever with Galician twentieth-century art. Some painters had done this as a sign of friendship; others as payment for the mugs – there were no glasses here – that they had drunk on credit.

Near the oak casks stacked on the uneven floor, conversations had taken place between Álvaro Cunqueiro, Castroviejo, Blanco Amor and other eminent men. Their table talk was an oasis of distinction in the industrial greyness which back then was expanding to the four corners of the town.

The writer Borobó, in one of his chronicles, had dreamed up a fable about the end of the halcyon days. Apparently the Lord, who of course knew that salmon had become extinct in Galician rivers, had invited Don Álvaro to dine at a higher table. Unable to resist a freebie, the usual crowd had come along with the great writer. And to lubricate the banquet they had requested wine from on high. The story goes that Eligio, with so many friends at the party, had no other option than to go and pour it himself. The details after that are not clear, and Eligio certainly never came back to tell his version, but it is said he didn't go up in the best of moods.

In any case, with Eligio in heaven, the bar passed to his

son-in-law, Carlos, without any trouble and without losing any of the former owner's spirit or the enlightened atmosphere it had acquired in Eligio's lifetime. True, the wine no longer cured you of the flu, but the culprits were the winemakers of the area rather than the soul of the place. The mugs were still white china, and the benches the same strong wood as always. A series of small riveted plaques memorialised the eminent regulars.

ↅ

It had gone twelve when the inspector checked his mobile. He realised it had been some time since he had received a call that made him rush out into the night. Then he asked for another mug of wine.

Cowering

On 13 May it felt like summer. The bright morning light came in through a window, filling the room at the police station. Rafael Estévez was sitting on a chair and going through a sheaf of papers. A woman, in silence, looked at him from across the table.

'María de Castro Rasposo, a resident of Canido, Vigo, widowed, sixty-four years old.'

'A youthful sixty-four,' she qualified.

'Is that more or less than sixty-four?' asked Estévez.

Inspector Caldas, who was standing nearby, checking the contents of a folder, put in:

'Please, Rafael, let's focus on the statement.'

The huge officer obeyed with a heavy sigh.

'María, yesterday, 12 May, you declared that you arrived at Reigosa's flat like any other day, at around three in the afternoon, and that you let yourself in with your own key. According to the statement, Reigosa gave you the key about two years ago, when you started working for him.'

The officer paused, seeking the woman's agreement. She made a signal with her head that he interpreted as a nod.

'You went up to the top floor, which is the one you normally clean first,' Estévez went on reading, 'is that right?'

'It depends, sometimes I do and sometimes I don't.'

'OK,' said Estévez, sternly staring at the woman, 'but do you usually clean the top floor first?'

'Often enough I do.'

Estévez was beginning to get impatient.

'Let's get this clear, ma'am. Did you clean the top floor first the day you found Reigosa dead?'

'I already told you I did, officer. You don't have to shout for me to understand,' she added, lifting a hand to her ear.

'Am I shouting?' Estévez sought the inspector's gaze.

Caldas kindly asked him to lower his voice. He really was surprised at how easily Estévez lost his temper, with barely any incitement.

'Let's try and make some progress here,' said Estévez, going back to his papers. 'It was half an hour after entering the flat, when you opened the door to the bedroom in order to clean it, that you found the late Mr Reigosa gagged and tied to the headboard of his bed. At that moment you left the house to go and call for help.'

The officer made another pause to look at the woman and obtain confirmation of what he'd just said.

'Is that so?' he asked.

María de Castro seemed more interested in the floor, where her gaze was fixed, than in the policeman's question.

'Is that so?' Estévez asked again, more loudly.

The woman stared at him in silence.

'Was that how it was?' repeated Estévez, prepared not to budge until he'd had an answer.

'More or less,' replied María de Castro.

'How do you mean "more or less"? Did it or did it not happen the way I'm saying?' insisted Estévez, more and more impatient.

'It might have been roughly the way you describe it,' said María de Castro at last.

'How might it have been roughly that way? This is your actual statement.' Estévez went back to the first paragraph, pointed at it and said: 'This is you, right, "María de Castro Rasposo, resident of Canido, Vigo, widowed..."?'

'Officer,' Caldas called him to order.

'Inspector, I'm only trying to get the lady to tell me if it was the way it says here. For fuck's sake, it's not a trick question.'

'It was pretty much as it says there, yes,' said María.

'Well, say it then. That's all I'm asking you.'

The woman shrugged.

'So you can also confirm you left the flat in search of the caretaker and, not finding him, went to the sentry box at the entrance of the island to warn the security guard who controls the bridge access,' proceeded Estévez, putting down the papers on the table once he finished. 'Is that right?'

A slight swing of the head was all he got in the way of an answer, but he interpreted it as an affirmative, and asked:

'María, did you see anything odd in the flat?'

'Odd?'

'Yes, odd, out of the ordinary,' repeated Estévez, irritated. 'Beside the fact that Reigosa was dead, of course. Did you see anything unusual, weird, strange, curious, anything at all that caught your attention? Anything along those lines?'

'Well I don't know,' she hesitated. 'I mean, something that may have caught my attention . . . no, I don't think so.'

Rafael turned to his superior, who was still on his feet, his back resting against the furthermost wall from the table.

'Inspector, when this lady tells me "I don't think so", does she actually mean "no"?'

'Yes indeed,' she replied.

Estévez turned back towards the woman, who held his gaze a few seconds and then scornfully looked away to the window.

'You'd better carry on yourself, chief,' said Estévez, standing up. He was throwing in the towel.

The inspector nodded and took a few steps in the room, holding up the folder in one hand and his second cigarette of the day in the other. The woman seemed to take no notice of him, so he approached the window, thus shielding her from the morning light.

'María, what I have here is a lophoscopic report,' he said in a calm voice, showing her the folder.

'A what?'

'The fingerprints report. That's a technique that allows us to identify the fingerprints that we find at a certain place.'

The frown on her face indicated that the explanation had not been enough. But she said:

'I see.'

'Do you remember that we took your fingerprints yesterday?'

'I remember a bit,' answered the woman.

'Since fingerprints are unique to every person, once we obtain them we can establish in all confidence who's been at a certain place and identify which things they've touched.'

'And?' María de Castro seemed positive that the conversation had little to do with her.

'Yours appeared all over the flat,' Caldas informed her.

'Mine?' She seemed surprised.

'Your very own fingerprints, María, they've appeared at the flat of the late Mr Reigosa's,' clarified the inspector, wriggling his own fingers.

'Well, I work there,' she said, 'I guess that's why...'

Caldas chose to ignore the reply and pressed on:

'The thing is, the glasses were covered with your fingerprints too, María,' he said softly.

'The glasses?'

'Do you know which ones I mean?' asked Inspector Caldas.

'Well, I know of lots of glasses,' she replied vaguely.

'In particular, I mean the ones that were sitting on the coffee table in the living room of Mr Reigosa's flat,' Caldas clarified. 'Do you remember the glasses we are referring to now?'

The woman rubbed her chin.

'Glasses... I don't know.'

'The glasses had gin in them and your fingerprints clearly stamped all over, María,' he said, raising his voice slightly. 'Fingerprints that ruined the rest of the prints we might have found there.'

María de Castro gave a start.

'Of course, the glasses!' She finally remembered. 'I had a

drink to steady myself. You know, after the shock of finding Mr Luis in such a horrible state. Did you not hear your partner say that it was me who found the body?'

'María, it's unlikely that you'll find yourself involved in a mess like this ever again, but if out of some strange coincidence it should happen, please do not touch anything! If you need to have a tipple, go to a bar, but faced with a dead person, leave everything as it is.'

'I only wanted...'

Caldas was not going to accept her excuses.

'You messed up the only lead we might have had on the identity of the person who shared the last hours of Reigosa's life. Do you realise how important that is?' he asked, again looking at his report, making her withdraw into her chair, seeking the support of its back.

During the inspection of Reigosa's flat a good number of fingerprints had been found, but the lophoscopic report confirmed that nearly all of them were either the dead man's or María de Castro Raposo's.

The only different one was a print on the bottom of one of the glasses left on the living-room coffee table. Unfortunately, Raposo's hands had damaged it considerably, and although the police had managed to salvage a fragment of the print, it wasn't quite enough to feed it into the police computerised archive for a match. Computers didn't work with fragments. They behaved just as Estévez did: they wanted all or nothing, and there were no such things as half measures for them.

If a suspect emerged they would have to manually compare his or her fingerprints with the small part they had salvaged from the glass – provided they obtained a court order to take them in the first place.

What seemed most surprising to Inspector Caldas was that no prints had been found in the bedroom, which seemed to confirm that the killer had taken the trouble of covering up his traces before leaving the flat. He was rather impressed that someone should have stayed to clean up while Reigosa, no doubt still alive, lay gagged on his bed with his hands tied to the headboard. It must have taken quite a lot of guts not to feel intimidated by the dying man's tormented blue eyes.

⤸

'Are you going to accuse me of having a small drink, inspector?' asked María de Castro, learning she had spoiled a piece of evidence.

Caldas shook his head and left the report on the table.

'Can I go, then?' she asked, visibly relieved.

The woman grabbed her bag, which was near the table on the floor, and put it on the table, awaiting the inspector's instructions. Now she knew she wasn't going to be punished, she tried to restore her challenged moral integrity: 'Besides, I only drank what was left in one of the glasses.'

'Tell her we found her prints on both of them,' Estévez said to his boss.

'Well, maybe I did drink from both. I can't remember everything, I'm sixty-four years old.'

'That's OK,' said Caldas, bringing the matter to a close and inviting her to leave.

Rafael Estévez, on the other hand, was unable to remain silent, as his DNA did not include his superior's Galician patience:

'We've also found your prints all over the gin bottle and all the rest of the liquor bottles in the kitchen.'

'I'm a cleaning lady. My job is to pick up things and clean them,' replied María de Castro, offended. 'Have you tried cleaning anything without touching it, officer?'

The police officer approached the table at which the woman was still sitting.

'Listen, lady, I won't have you making fun of me,' he warned her, pointing his index finger at her.

Caldas dragged him aside and asked the terrified woman

to leave. He had to help her up, as she was so frightened she was almost cowering under the table.

As soon as she was up she obeyed the inspector. She left the room in a hurry without taking her eyes off Estévez.

'Are you out of your mind?' said Caldas, once she was out the door. 'Do you want us both to get a bollocking?'

'But if I didn't stop that old bag in her tracks, she would've tried to convince us that she was a teetotaller,' Estévez justified himself.

'It doesn't matter, Rafael. You can have a go at her all you want, that won't get the fingerprints back. Can't you be practical for a change? We only needed her to confirm what she'd said on her statement.'

'And what do you think, chief, has she confirmed it?'

'In a way,' said Caldas.

'In a way – has she or hasn't she?'

'In a way, Rafael,' replied Caldas tersely. Some people need to learn how to listen.

The inspector put out his cigarette, picked up the report and made off for his office, leaving Estévez alone in the room. On the way over his mobile rang. Doctor Guzmán Barrio's initial results were in.

Poison

'Formaldehyde?' asked Caldas.

'Formaldehyde. Also known as formalin.'

'But isn't that a preservative?'

'It is indeed. One of its main uses is the preservation of tissue. It has to be diluted in water in a concentration of around thirty-seven per cent. In smaller concentrations it is used as a disinfectant.'

'Which means?' asked Caldas, still unable to understand what the musician's death had to do with the doctor's explanation.

'Formaldehyde,' continued the doctor 'is a dangerous product, a very toxic gas. It has irritant and allergenic effects,' Guzmán paused. 'It even has a component that can be carcinogenic.'

'Doctor, are you suggesting they dipped his balls in formaldehyde until he got genital cancer?' asked Estévez sceptically.

'Don't be silly,' replied Barrio. 'No one's said anything about dipping his parts in formalin.'

Nevertheless, Caldas's face betrayed doubts.

'I'm sorry, Guzmán, but I'm not sure I understand where you're going with this. If they didn't pour formaldehyde on his skin, what did they do?'

'They injected it,' said the doctor.

'What?' Caldas wasn't sure he'd heard right.

'Someone injected formaldehyde into Reigosa's genitals. A solution of thirty-seven per cent formaldehyde.'

'God,' exclaimed Estévez. 'How is that possible?'

'It was precisely here,' said Barrio approaching the trolley where Reigosa's body lay. He uncovered his naked body and stretched the skin of the dead man's penis. 'This little dot here is the mark left by the needle. Can you see the hole?'

'Fuck, I can't see it and I don't particularly want to,' protested Estévez, who bent his huge body in two and thus made off for the door. 'You don't mind if I go and get some air, do you? The inspector can fill me in on the news later.'

Rafael Estévez went out of the room, leaving his boss and the doctor in front of Reigosa's body. Leo Caldas bent down to observe the minuscule perforation that Barrio had pointed out. Certainly, it wasn't pleasant to look at the saxophonist's disgusting member once again.

'I don't get it, Guzmán. Didn't we say formaldehyde was a preservative?'

'Formaldehyde dries tissues up. If you put a dead body in formaldehyde, it doesn't decay, right? But, on the other hand, if you put it into a *living* body, it absorbs all the liquid the body might have,' the doctor inhaled sharply.

'Crikey,' whispered Caldas, feeling an inner shiver.

'When they injected it, everything shrivelled up,' continued Guzmán Barrio. 'Because, once the formaldehyde is in, nothing escapes drying out: capillaries, tissues, nothing... Don't forget that most of the human body, nearly eighty per cent of it, is made of water, and that down there,' he said gesturing towards the musician's genitals, 'there's not even a bone that might slow the shrivelling one bit.'

Leo Caldas remained silent for a few moments, gazing at the astonishing effect produced in Luis Reigosa's abdominal area.

'So whoever did this knew they were killing him?'

'What do you think?' replied Barrio, Galician style.

'Couldn't it have been a situation that got out of hand?' asked Caldas, unable to imagine a mind capable of dreaming up this way of killing.

'I doubt it,' assured Barrio, shaking his head. 'I think they knew enough, at the very least, to predict the outcome. Whoever planned an execution such as this, by toxic injection, had to have enough medical training to know that you cannot go on living with your main blood vessels deteriorated to such an extent. This is worthy of Caligula.'

Caldas was astonished at Guzmán Barrio's explanations. The method seemed to point to a vengeful lover, but at the same time it seemed too cruel for a simple personal vendetta.

'Formaldehyde has an isquemic component, so upon injection it must have caused extreme pain,' continued Barrio, who seemed impressed by his own explanations. 'To give you an idea, it would be the kind of pain a diabetic suffers when losing a leg – a tremendous septic shock. Now try and picture that in an area with so many blood vessels as the male genitalia, which have the capacity to triplicate their volume when the blood flow reaches them. I should think such cruel torture was planned.'

'I see.' Caldas would rather not imagine the scene, and he was not paying much attention to the detail the doctor supplied.

'If he'd been found alive, it would've been imperative to amputate his penis and testicles. This poor man would've been forced to urinate through a catheter from his groin or, even worse, directly from his kidneys.'

Barrio stopped the lecture to gaze at the huge swelling covering nearly a third of Reigosa's body.

'In fact, I don't think he would've pulled through even if we'd got here only a minute after the poisoning, Leo. The femoral artery is too close, and look at his legs! We couldn't have done anything but pray for him as he writhed in agony. I don't think there would've been a way to save him.'

Leo preferred to avoid the more scabrous matters for now. He knew from experience that getting involved at a personal level skewed the investigation and damaged his efficiency as a hunter. The case was becoming a tangled skein of information, and he had to concentrate on finding the end of the thread that would allow him to pull and unravel it.

'And what can you tell me about the time of death?'

'Between ten and twelve the day before yesterday. That I know for a fact.'

Leo Caldas looked at the lifeless body, with its horrendous blackness. He was still perplexed at the gruesome way they'd killed him.

'Guzmán, who would have access to formaldehyde?'

'At a hospital? Well, a doctor, a nurse, an orderly, a medical student.' Barrio threw his arms in the air, indicating that any other person who worked in a hospital fell into the category of those who did.

Yet Caldas could not quite comprehend that something capable of producing the effects observed in the saxophonist's body might be almost within anyone's reach.

'But if it's as toxic as you say, it must be under tight control.'

'I don't think so. It's not hard to come by, and for the moment we're only talking hospitals. If I'm not mistaken, it's used for many other purposes, not only as a preservative.'

Guzmán Barrio excused himself from the room, and a few moments later returned with a chemistry book in his hands.

'Here it is – formaldehyde. In addition, it's used in industrial products such as fertilisers, paints, adhesives, abrasives...' Barrio shut the book. 'As you can see it's pretty common.'

Leo recalled a film he'd seen some time before. The protagonist was an overweight nurse who held a writer captive at a mountain refuge for a snowy winter. The woman forced him to write a book just the way she liked it. And, each time she went out to buy food, she tied him to his bed to stop him running away. On one occasion, the nurse returned early to find the writer trying to free himself from his ties. As a punishment, and to make sure he wouldn't try to escape again, she hit his ankle with a sledge hammer, at the exact spot where she knew it would fracture.

'What are you thinking of?' asked Guzmán Barrio.

Caldas came back to reality.

'That it's quite unlikely that an adhesive or paint manufacturer might know the effects of injecting formaldehyde in someone's penis.'

'I agree. In fact, I myself didn't quite know about its effect inside a living body,' confessed Guzmán Barrio. 'So I'd say it had to be someone with very precise medical knowledge.'

'Hospital staff?'

Barrio shook his head, signalling he didn't quite think so.

'Most hospital staff have no idea that formaldehyde can produce this kind of toxaemia. I'd be inclined to think of some specialist, someone who deals with the substance, who's used to experimenting or working with it on a regular basis. Then again, hospitals are full of morons.'

'I'm so relieved to hear that,' said Leo Caldas, while he remembered the sadistic nurse in the film.

'No, I mean it. If people knew the psychological profiles of some of my colleagues they'd go for a cure straight to the butcher's.'

'It must be like everywhere else.'

'Don't be so sure.'

'Right.' Banter didn't contribute anything now, and the inspector didn't want to leave the autopsy room without some kind of lead.

'Do you know who the suppliers are?'

'Of formaldehyde?'

Caldas nodded, thinking that had Estévez been present he wouldn't have hesitated to counter this with some choice expression of his own.

'Here we order it from Riofarma, as it's the closest lab.'

'Is it produced there?' answered Caldas with some surprise. He was actually familiar with the company.

'The one I get is,' confirmed Barrio. 'But formaldehyde is produced in many labs. As I said, it's easy to make. Since it's pretty much the same anywhere, I choose to buy it in the region, and so save myself any shipping costs. By and large, everyone does the same with these kinds of products.'

It was a new lead, Leo Caldas thought.

'Thanks for all the information,' he said, by way of good-bye. 'When will you finish?'

'The post-mortem is finished. All that's left is to send the report to the court and the police station, and call the family to let them know they can come and collect the body,' the doctor explained. 'I think they want to bury him right away.'

'Do you happen to know where?'

Barrio said he didn't.

'If you like, I can find out and call you on your mobile later?'

'Thanks. And let me know if there's any news.'

Caldas walked over to the door. When he came out into the corridor, he recalled another image from the film with the fat nurse: now she was walking down a corridor with a syringe in her hand.

'Leo, Leo!' the door of the autopsy room opened, and Guzmán Barrio asked him to come back.

'Is there anything else?' asked Caldas, once back in.

'Yes, sorry, with all that talk about formaldehyde I almost forgot to tell you about the rest,' Barrio blurted out. 'There's another thing, and if I'm not mistaken it might be relevant to the investigation. Remember yesterday, how surprised you were that Reigosa might have had sexual intercourse before he was killed?'

The inspector replied he did, anxiously awaiting the doctor's conclusions in that respect.

'Well, I wasn't able to find any evidence indicating that Reigosa had sex the night he died,' informed Guzmán Barrio, 'but I wanted to ask you something – do you know if he was gay?'

'Reigosa?'

'During my examination I found signs that point in that direction.'

'Are you sure?' asked Leo Caldas, as he saw the fat nurse with the syringe disappear from the suspects' line-up.

'I'm only saying it's reasonable to suppose so, Leo. As you know, the ignorant assert while the wise think things over.'

As the inspector left, he remembered what Rafael Estévez had said on the eighteenth storey of the Toralla tower about the saxophonist's sexual orientation. Sometimes, an ignorant man can be assertive and right.

Solvent

A jazz saxophonist, Luis Reigosa was single and lived alone. His mother lived in a small house on the seashore by the Pontevedera inlet, in the fishing village of Bueu, which was also his place of birth. He didn't have any known siblings or a known father. According to the security guards at the entrance to Toralla Island, he was a quiet man, even if he lived mostly by night. He played the sax with his band four days a week at the Grial, a bar on the edge of the city's old quarter. There were three members in the band, including Reigosa himself. The other two were the Irish bass player Arthur O'Neal and the pianist Iria Ledo. Reigosa had also taught as a supply teacher at the municipal conservatory of Vigo.

It was a beautiful day, bright and clear, without a cloud in the sky, and Rafael Estévez drove in silence. Leo Caldas spent the drive examining a report drawn up by Officer Ferro from forensics. Its many stapled sheets recorded some preliminary considerations, impressions put forward by a few neighbours, the caretaker of the building, María de Castro, and the security guard who was on duty on the night of the crime. The guard remembered seeing Reigosa's car driving on to the island, but he didn't recall anyone else being there with him. In any case, he made it a rule not to pry into the identity of guests. He'd seen the vehicle leave a few hours later, in the small hours, and had assumed it was Reigosa who was driving. He blamed this on the darkness and the rain that night.

The car had not reappeared.

The report also contained the lophoscopic analysis and the results of the first inspection of the flat. Forensics ruled out the possibility that Reigosa might have been tied up and gagged after being killed, and marked the time of death at around eleven p.m. on 11 May. On the whole, it wasn't the most exhaustive report Caldas had read, and it barely contributed anything new, but it was still better than nothing. Clara Barcia's conclusions were still pending; she would take another couple of days. Caldas was confident that her meticulousness at combing the scene would open new avenues of investigation, but for the moment he couldn't find a clear way forward. In his mind, he went over what he had: the small part of a fingerprint that was impossible to match with any prints stored in the police files; a commonly used chemical product as a weapon; and the certainty that the murderer must have had quite an advanced degree of medical knowledge. It was also quite likely that the murderer was a man. A homosexual man.

Caldas took the portrait he'd commandeered at Reigosa's flat out of the pocket of his jacket. Once again he had the impression he was missing something. He couldn't put his finger on it, but a little voice inside him told him a piece didn't quite fit in that puzzle. He knew that feeling, and trusted his instinct. He was sure that, no matter how small it was, whatever was hiding at the back of his mind now would suddenly come to light at a later stage.

He tilted his head back, returned the picture to his pocket and closed his eyes.

The small village of Porriño was in the valley of the Louro river, where it flowed towards the Miño. It was some ten kilometres away from Vigo. The southbound motorway, to Portugal, and the eastbound, to Madrid, went past near the village, which was growing at the same speed as the granite mountains around it were being quarried.

A few years back, as a consequence of the quarrying boom, a large industrial park had been built in the region. Reasonable land prices, good road links and tax exemptions had attracted many companies to Vigo.

⌒

The policemen left a few ships behind and got off the motorway. They went on along the main road until they reached a high fence that protected several hectares of land. A name was written in sober lettering over the gate at the entrance: 'Riofarma'.

The building housing the laboratory had retained the flavour of old companies: a certain air of mystery. The stone it was made of gave it a look of nobility and strength which was lacking in the new structures of the industrial area. After several decades, the company was still owned by the family of the founder, Lisardo Ríos.

⌒

'Good morning,' said a security guard as he approached the car.

Estévez sought help in the seat next to him.

'Ramón Ríos is expecting us. I'm Inspector Leo Caldas from the Vigo police station.'

'Inspector Leo Caldas?'

'Yes,' he confirmed.

'Are you really Leo Caldas, from *Patrol on the Air*?'

'The very same one,' confirmed Estévez, nodding appreciatively.

'Leo Caldas... I can't believe it, I never miss your show. Here in my box I always tune in to Radio Vigo.' The man stuck half his body out of the window and offered his hand. 'It's a misleading medium, radio, isn't it? I would have thought you were an older man.'

'I'm sorry to disappoint,' replied Caldas as he shook his hand. He still couldn't figure out how anyone could like the programme.

'I'm not disappointed at all,' said the security guard without letting go of his hand. 'It's a pleasure to meet you, inspector.'

'Can we come in now?' asked Caldas, when he considered his lower arm had been sufficiently shaken.

The guard opened the gate, revealing the beautiful gardens that surrounded the building of the laboratory.

'It's been a pleasure,' he shouted enthusiastically as they went through.

'All the best,' replied the inspector with a forced smile.

'Funny what fame achieves, right, chief?' Estévez commented once they'd cleared the gate.

'What do you mean, fame?'

'Oh, no need to be humble in front of me, chief. You saw it – once he recognised you, he let us through straight away.'

'I'm not that well known. Besides, it's pretty normal not to stand in the way when the police want to come through.'

'Come on, inspector, you won't deny that people treat you completely differently because you're on the radio. When we're undercover, or when I go somewhere on my own, everyone looks annoyed. But if you identify yourself as the officer from *Patrol on the Air*, we instantly receive special treatment, as happened just now.'

'Firstly, I didn't identify myself as anything. Secondly, you won't receive any special treatment from people if you beat them up at the slightest provocation.'

'Don't lecture me on work ethics,' Estévez defended himself. 'We all have our methods. If you're not aware that your popularity is a plus, there's no reason to turn it against me. Your success is your own business.'

'Leave me alone, will you?' said Caldas, sensing that his assistant might be right. Despite his many years of service as a police officer, if anyone knew him it was because of that ridiculous radio programme, no matter how much he disliked being a part of it.

They got out of the car and made for the building. Ramón Ríos was waiting for them at the entrance.

⌣

Ramón Ríos had been Leo Caldas's schoolmate. Together they had learned many disparate things: that there was one sin graver than the others; that a goal scored from a penalty kick was a valid goal; that the derivative at a point equalled the slope of the line tangent to the graph of the function at that point... They had also heard Don José instructing them on extreme situations from the pulpit: for instance, if a terrorist is threatening a child's family with a machine gun and asks the child to trample on a consecrated wafer, the child need not trample on it, for if the terrorist were to follow through and shoot, the family would ascend into heaven, happy and whole, as martyrs. On some occasions, provided that Alba was part of the deal, Leo would have agreed with Don José's unorthodox theory. On most he wouldn't.

'Leo, you must be the only madman who comes to the lab when he wants to see me,' said Ríos, by way of greeting.

'Each to their own, you know.'

They greeted with a hug. Although they no longer saw each other on a regular basis, they still acknowledged a pleasant well of friendship left over from childhood, when, for different reasons, both had found it quite difficult to interact with other children.

'This time it's not a personal visit, but a matter related to your line of work,' said Leo Caldas, hinting at why he was there.

'My what? Are you sure you're OK?'

'Don't they pay you for coming here?' asked Leo.

'Only not to have me moping around the house,' replied Ríos, and looked at the expensive watch he sported on his left wrist. 'On a day like this, I'll be on the boat in half an hour at the latest.'

'Lucky for some,' said the inspector.

Ramón Ríos gestured in the direction of Estévez, who had lagged behind and was engrossed watching four young people in white coats manipulating a smoking green liquid.

'You've got yourself a gorilla?' he asked in a low voice.

'Rafael Estévez, my new assistant. He's only been in the city a few months. Rafael!' he called out.

'Quite a beast! I'm sure you're well protected,' muttered Ríos, winking at him in the same naughty manner he had as a child. 'I'd heard radio celebrities need bodyguards.'

'It must be that,' Caldas said tersely.

Estévez came over and said hello to Ríos.

'How's it going?'

'Well, losing quite a bit of hair. Otherwise I can't complain.'

'Rafael, this is Ramón Ríos,' said Caldas.

'A pleasure,' said Estévez, and pointed in the direction of the men in white coats. 'What are they doing?'

'The ones with the green smoke?'

Rafael Estévez nodded.

'I have no idea,' replied Ríos, as if there were no other possible answer to the officer's question. 'I only know about stuff in my area, and not even much about that, to be honest. In my family the clever one was Grandpa Lisardo, who set up this joint. Nowadays, the really clever ones are my brother, my cousin and the cat. And, round here, no one's terribly clever either. In fact they're all pretty dumb,' he said, looking at a couple of employees coming down the corridor. 'The best brains go over to the competition. The thing is, since Zetiza was floated, it pays better than us.'

Estévez nodded slightly.

Ramón carried on with his speech.

'Anyway, I'm allergic to the lab myself, and that's why I'm here as little as possible. I often get these rashes, you know, which only heal with seawater and a nice breeze. I'm sure it's some kind of incompatibility between wine and one of the substances we produce here. Do you want to know something?' he asked, looking at Rafael Estévez.

'No, thank you,' replied the officer, who, after listening to the maelstrom of words Ríos was capable of, thought it more advisable not to take part in the conversation.

'Leo tells me you're not from round here.'

'No, sir, I'm from Zaragoza. Have you been there?'

'Do you say "sir" because I'm bald?'

'Pardon?' asked the officer.

'You can call me by my first name, young man. I may be ugly, but I'm not that old. See?' he said, opening his mouth wide. 'I still have all my teeth on this side.'

'There's no use trying, Ramón,' put in Caldas.

'As you like, but one starts with all that sir-business and ends up genuflecting, as we used to do at school.'

Ramón started walking along the corridor that abutted at the hall.

'Come this way, we'll carry on talking at the tennis court.'

Estévez stood bolted to his place, looking at the inspector in bewilderment.

'Where?'

'His office,' replied Leo Caldas, following Ríos.

～

Ramón Ríos had a huge office with walnut wood panelling. A Persian carpet covered nearly all the floor. On one side, in an area reserved for meetings, eight leather chairs surrounded a large conference table with a state-of-the-art telephone on its centre. On the other, by the window, an antique piece of furniture served as a desk. There was a sports newspaper open on it.

'Crikey, for someone who doesn't do any work here, it's not bad,' joked Caldas on coming in.

'I know,' admitted Ramón Ríos, taking a look around.

On several occasions Leo Caldas had witnessed how envious his schoolmates were of Ramón Ríos's way of casually talking about his opulent life. But Leo had never harboured such feelings himself; on the contrary, he valued Ríos's generous and faithful friendship. If there was something he would have wished for himself, it was Ríos's impetuous self-confidence, a far cry from his own natural shyness.

'Do sit down and tell me what miracle brings you gentlemen here,' said Ramón Ríos.

The policemen chose two of the chairs around the table and waited in silence for Ramón Ríos to take another one.

'Formaldehyde,' said Caldas tersely.

'Formaldehyde, how do you mean, formaldehyde?' asked Ríos. 'What can you possibly mean, Leo?'

'Formaldehyde is one of Riofarma's products and we'd like to know the names of your clients in the city.'

Ramón looked at Caldas as if he'd spoken in a foreign tongue.

'Well, we'll need to check that,' he replied at last, when he realised that his former schoolmate was being serious, and that formaldehyde really was the reason for his visit.

'By the way, Leo, how's your father these days?' he asked, pulling the cord of the telephone and dragging it towards himself.

'As always. A bit in his own world. We're having lunch tomorrow, but we haven't seen a lot of each other lately. Tomorrow we're meeting up because he must come to Vigo on some errand, but if it was up to him he'd never leave the vineyard.'

'I don't blame him. What's the wine like this year?'

'It seems to be top-notch in quality, but the old man complains that production has dropped. Apparently it rained at the wrong time. I don't know what the hell he means by the wrong time, but that's what he says. I think he actually likes to complain – but we're only in May and he's already sold half of this year's lot.'

'He sells it too well,' assured Ramón Ríos. 'Last year, when I wanted to order a few boxes, he was already out. And the year before that I couldn't taste it either.'

'Well, you know, it sells out in no time,' said Caldas, as if excusing his father.

Ríos nodded, and then said: 'When you see him tell him I'd like to sample a few bottles. Tell him to put aside as many as he can. Remind him I'm solvent if needs be.'

Leo smiled and pointed to the phone.

'I'll take care of the wine, you make that call.'

Ríos pressed one of the buttons of the fancy telephone, activating the loudspeaker so that all three could hear the conversation. The dialling tone rang clearly in the room.

He had to make several calls. First to ascertain that, as Caldas claimed, the laboratory owned by his family did produce formaldehyde. Then to find out which division produced it and so on. When he finally got the right number, there was a feminine voice at the other end.

'Good morning, Solutions and Concentrates, how can I help?'

'Good morning, Ramón Ríos here.'

'Don Ramón, what a surprise!' The woman faltered and tried to fix the comment that had just slipped out. 'I'm sorry, Don Ramón, what I meant was...'

'Don't worry, it would have been strange not to be surprised,' he reassured her, tipping a wink at the inspector. 'Who am I speaking to?'

'Carmen Iglesias.'

'Hi Carmen. I'm trying to find out something about one of our products. Would that be possible?'

'That's what we're here for, Don Ramón,' replied the woman, obviously eager to please.

'Do we produce formaldehyde?' asked Ríos.

'It depends what you mean.'

'I understand your division produces it,' explained Ríos.

'We don't actually produce the substance, Don Ramón, but we do work with it. We buy it from the manufacturer and here, in Solutions and Concentrates, we treat it and bottle it according to the different ways our clients might use it,' clarified Carmen Iglesias.

'The thing is, I'm here with some friends who'd like to know a few details about the process. Would you mind helping them?'

'By all means, Don Ramón.'

'I'll put them on in a moment, Carmen, but before that let

me tell you that your voice sounds very...' Ramón Ríos
trailed off, searching for the right word, 'charming.'

'Thank you, Don Ramón,' said the woman, amused.

Caldas bent over the telephone.

'Good morning, Carmen, this is Inspector Caldas.'

'From the radio?' Carmen's voice betrayed emotion.

'You see?' said Estévez just before Caldas gave him a with-
ering look.

Caldas accepted the woman's congratulations, and her
assurances that in Solutions and Concentrates they never
missed a programme of *Patrol on the Air*. But as soon as he
saw an opening he limited himself to the subject that had
taken them to the laboratory.

'Carmen, would it be possible to obtain a list of the clients
who buy formaldehyde from you?'

'In all concentrations?' she asked.

'In all concentrations?' repeated Caldas, looking at Ramón
Ríos in search of an explanation.

Ríos shrugged his shoulders and bent over the phone.

'Carmen, would you be kind enough to explain to the
inspector and me what you mean about the concentrations?'
he asked.

'It's quite simple, Don Ramón, every formaldehyde
solution is a different product, used for different things. We
have solutions ranging from a concentration of eight per
cent formaldehyde, as used by paper manufacturers and tan-
ners, up to solutions with thirty-seven per cent formaldehyde, which is what we normally send to hospitals, and then
we have...'

'I need the second one, Carmen,' interrupted Caldas. 'Is it
possible to know which medical centres you provide with
thirty-seven per cent formaldehyde solutions? I'm particularly interested in your clients here in Vigo.'

'Of course, inspector. The best thing would be to speak
directly to Isidro Freire, the representative for the area. He's
in charge of the sales of all our products in Vigo.'

'Would it be too much to ask you to transfer me to Mr Freire?' asked Caldas.

'Not at all, inspector, but Isidro had an appointment and I saw him leave a moment ago. I don't think he's even had time to reach his car. If you like I can call him on his mobile and ask him to wait.'

'If that's not a problem...'

'Of course it isn't, inspector. I'll call him right away.'

'Many thanks, you've been very kind.'

'You're welcome, inspector. Now if you don't mind, I'll leave you so I can make that call.'

'Just another thing, Carmen,' interrupted Ramón Ríos, who never missed a chance.

'Yes, Don Ramón?'

'I was wondering how old is the owner of that lovely voice?'

'Thanks, Don Ramón, I'm about to turn twenty-seven.'

Judging by the woman's honeyed intonation, Caldas understood she hadn't minded his friend's comment in the slightest.

Ramón Ríos shook the policemen's hands, disconnected the loudspeaker, and unhooked the receiver.

'I'm just curious, Carmen, do you like sailing?'

Obstinacy

It was coming up to one o'clock in the afternoon, and it was quite hot when the policemen left the Riofarma building. The lawn surrounding it smelled of recently mown grass. The sprinklers cast water as they turned slowly in one direction and then, upon reaching the end of their curve, quickly went back to the starting point.

Leo Caldas and Rafael Estévez went round the laboratory following a path of flagstones sunk in the thick grass. They'd been told that Isidro Freire would be waiting for them in the car park at the back.

As they turned the corner, they saw a man playing with a small black dog whose coat of long black curls resembled a Rastafarian's dreadlocks. The puppy ran towards them, its fur swaying this way and that, and hurled himself at Estévez's feet.

'Get the fuck out of here, you mongrel!'

He kicked the dog away, and a ball of black dreadlocks was suddenly aloft.

'Rafa, don't be so horrible, he's only a puppy,' said Inspector Caldas.

'Puppy schmuppy, chief. Do you think he doesn't have any teeth?' replied Estévez, convinced he was in the right. 'I don't know what dogs see in me, but they always come and annoy me,' he added. 'I can be in the middle of a crowd, and if there's a hound on the loose it'll surely single me out.'

'It can't be the way you treat them.'

As soon as the puppy scrambled up, he charged the officer's shoes.

'You see what I mean, inspector, he's practically *asking* to be kicked.'

'Rafael, don't do anything, please – here comes the owner,' said Caldas as the man who'd been playing with the dog approached quickly.

'This shitty dog will end up ruining my new shoes,' said Estévez, as he reluctantly allowed the puppy to play with them.

'Pipo, come, Pipo!' called the man as he approached. 'Go on, Pipo, go with Daddy.'

Estévez pushed the dog with his foot, launching him a few metres in the direction of his owner.

'I'm sorry,' said the man, 'Pipo's been in the car all morning, and there's no stopping him when you let him out. But as soon as his adrenaline wears off a bit he'll obey me again.'

To Caldas it didn't look like the dog would ever obey, whether pumped full of adrenaline or heavily sedated.

'It doesn't matter,' he said. 'Are you Isidro Freire?'

The man picked Pipo up and held him.

'Are you Don Ramón's friends, the gentlemen from the radio?'

Rafael Estévez let out a chuckle, and Caldas explained himself.

'I don't think they passed on the right information. We are indeed friends of Ramón's, but we don't exactly come from the radio. We're police officers from the Vigo station. I'm Inspector Caldas and your dog's friend is Officer Rafael Estévez.'

'From the police station? Is anything wrong?'

Caldas noticed the man trembled slightly as he spoke. He had read many years ago, in Camilo José Cela's *The Hive*, that a slight tremor of the lower lip was a giveaway of fear. He had often witnessed the accuracy of the Nobel Prize-winning Galician writer's observations.

'Don't worry, Mr Freire,' Caldas reassured him. 'It has nothing to do with you. At least not with you personally.'

Isidro Freire breathed out in relief.

'We'd only like a list of your clients in Vigo, those who

buy the thirty-seven per cent formaldehyde solution from Riofarma,' clarified the inspector. 'We've been told you're the right person to get that information from.'

'Of course, Vigo is my area, and formaldehyde one of the products I sell,' confirmed Isidro Freire, brooding over the matter for a moment. 'I haven't got many buyers for clinical formaldehyde, but I'd like to check my records to be absolutely sure. Would you mind walking over to my car to get my diary?' he asked, pointing towards the car park, and putting the puppy back on the ground.

'Of course not,' replied Caldas as they started walking.

Isidro Freire was a little over thirty and taller than Caldas; he combed his short brown hair with a parting that seemed branded on his skull. He was wearing dark trousers, a light blue shirt and black leather shoes. Most probably he'd left his jacket and tie in the car, as the heat didn't allow unnecessary extras, but even so he looked handsome. Caldas thought he must be among those men who are successful with women.

A few steps behind, Pipo insisted on fighting Rafael Estévez's ankles, and Estévez went on trying to kick him. When Leo Caldas realised the danger the animal was in, he alerted his owner with a flick of his head.

'Pipo, leave the gentleman alone!' ordered Isidro Freire, and crouched down to push away the obstinate little dog. He lifted him up, carried him for a bit, and dropped him gently in front of them.

They walked to the car along the flagstone path, and Pipo broke into a run on the grass.

'I'd never seen a dog with such long curls,' commented the inspector. 'What breed is he?'

'Pipo? He's a Puli, inspector.'

Leo Caldas had no idea what that was.

'I see.'

'A sheep dog, a Hungarian shepherd.'

Pipo dashed about and then chose a sprinkler as his next target.

'Come here, Pipo, you're going to get all wet!' ordered Freire, apparently convinced that the animal understood his every word.

The little dog obeyed him only after getting completely soaked. Then he came back running. A set of perfectly small white teeth shone in the black muzzle of that canine Bob Marley. There was something hanging from it.

'Pipo, what have you got in your mouth?' asked Freire.

It was Rafael Estévez who answered from behind.

'My bloody shoelace.'

Sweating

Rafael Estévez licked his fingers and grabbed another one. For Leo Caldas these were the first sardines of the season; for Estévez the first ever.

They hadn't planned to eat here, but Guzmán Barrio's call, informing them of the time of Reigosa's funeral, had forced them to change their arrangements. They decided not to return to Vigo, but grab a bite en route and attend the funeral shortly afterwards.

It had been Ríos who recommended the Porriño restaurant, though he himself had opted for deep-sea fishing rather than join them in sampling the sardines. Rafael Estévez had insisted on braving the heat by sitting under the vines, to one side of the barbecue where the fish and some unpeeled potatoes were being slowly grilled over the corn-cob embers.

'These are great, chief,' said Estévez with his mouth full. 'To be honest, I thought it was a bit disgusting to eat fish with your fingers, but you were right, they taste better this way.'

'I told you.'

Rafael left the backbone on his plate and grabbed another.

'Don't you think they're a bit small, inspector?'

'As we say here, "*a muller e a sardiña, pequeniña*" – women and sardines are best when small.'

'I'm not sure I agree.'

'I thought you wouldn't,' muttered Caldas, helping himself to a piece of potato and placing the sardine on top of it, so that the potato would soak up the grease and salt of the fish.

He wiped his hands in a paper napkin, reached for the wine jug and refilled his glass. The house white a bit sour, but he welcomed its freshness nevertheless. He then lifted the fish with both hands, by its head and tail, and bit into the salty meat with relish. Next he placed the half-eaten fish on his plate and mashed the sardine-drenched piece of potato with his fork. This he spread on a piece of corn-bread, and took a bite. Finally he went back to the sardine and dispatched the other half. After a year without tasting them, their flavour was glorious.

Once they'd had their fill of sardines, they rounded off with local cheese; Rafael Estévez pulled his stool near one of the stone pillars that held up the vine, and leaned his back against it. He was sweating profusely even though the vine leaves shielded him from the sun.

'So much for Galicia not being very hot,' he protested, fanning himself with his hand.

'It's cooler inside,' retorted Leo, as he remembered it had been Estévez's idea to sit out.

'Oh, don't tell me it isn't wonderful out here in the shade,' said Estévez, defending his choice. 'I sweat because I'm a bit overweight... If only there was a little breeze, it would be perfect.'

Then Estévez lifted his eyes to the vine and remarked:

'Quite a brainwave they had placing the tables under the plants. What are those little balls, by the way?'

'Those little balls up there?'

'Please, don't start, inspector. If we're both looking up and I ask you about the little balls, I must be referring to the balls we see up there, not mine...'

'They're white grapes.'

'But how do you know they're white? They look dark green to me.'

'The bunches are still full of chlorophyll. At the beginning all grapes are green. Then, as they mature, white grapes start turning yellow, and red ones go a sort of purple.'

'And how do you know these are white ones?'

'Because I know. Nearly all the wine in the area is white, and then the plant is a *treixadura*. See the leaves?'

Estévez looked up.

'Is that one of your rhetorical questions or do you think I'm going blind because of the sardines?'

'Just drop it, will you? I'm telling you they're white. You can believe me if you want, and if not you can come back during the harvest and see for yourself.'

The conversation about wine made Caldas's thoughts turn to his father, who found it harder and harder to leave his world of vines to visit the city. Caldas hadn't seen him for weeks and hadn't had the heart to refuse when his father called to suggest they meet up. However, he wasn't sure he'd enjoy having lunch with him the following day. Once again he'd have to go on his own, without Alba and without answers.

⊷

Once they finished their coffee, Caldas checked his watch.

'What time did Barrio say the funeral was?'

'Five o'clock, I think. You spoke to him.'

Caldas asked for the bill as the waiter went by.

'We'd better be going, Rafael, it'll take us almost an hour to get to Bueu.'

'God, inspector, always driving around, like a bloody cab.'

The cortège

A woman in mourning was crying. Two others, also in black, held her to stop her from falling, though no one tried to console her. Nearby, a group of grieving children looked at Reigosa's mother.

The small cemetery occupied a rectangle adjoining a Romanic chapel. It was at the top of a hill sprinkled with the yellow flowers of the *retama* bushes. Four crosses surmounted the corners where the crenellated walls of the cemetery converged, and an iron gate closed it off. Caldas and Estévez had had to take a badly paved road to reach the top, a promontory from which one could admire the *rías* of Pontevedra and Aldán. The tide was low, and the wet sand of the beaches shone brightly in the sun.

'It's lovely,' Estévez had commented as they arrived.

'Yes, it's a beautiful day.'

'I mean the cemetery, it's quite lovely.'

'The cemetery?'

'Yes, here all cemeteries are. They have a certain something. I don't know if it's the stone covered in moss, the crosses or what, but they're not like that where I come from.'

Caldas stopped to take a look. He'd never noticed the beauty of cemeteries before. He thought one could only find painful memories in them, but had to recognise that Estévez was right: this one was beautiful.

At its centre were two mausoleums with small outside chapels. They were surrounded by some thirty graves, though most tombs were housed in sepulchres or *nichos*, deep recesses in the cemetery walls, which had four levels and looked a bit like a honeycomb. Most of these had flowers – some wilted and some fresh – and the odd lit candle. The *nichos* in one of the walls were all empty, as if reminding the visitor of his destiny.

The policemen stayed behind the mausoleum, not too near the cortège. They could hear the mother's wails as the gravedigger, atop a ladder, sealed off the tomb in the wall with cement. He smoothed out the mix again and again, as if he wanted to prove his sepulchral expertise. Each lick of the trowel wrenched a new cry from the mother, who refused to abandon her son there. The man applied so many coats that Caldas had to restrain himself from shouting at him to finish up. He wondered whether the man would do it as slowly on a rainy day.

It was not a large cortège. On a rough calculation, Leo would have said forty people. The mother and other women, neighbours or relatives of the deceased, were at the front. Some of the townsmen, who had stayed smoking outside the church during the memorial, had now approached the tomb. The children must be Luis Reigosa's pupils: the inspector had seen a van parked outside, which had a sticker from the Vigo conservatory.

The bohemian-looking group couldn't be from the area. Caldas thought they must be Reigosa's fellow jazz players. Their city ways stuck out a mile. A man with red hair, as tall as Estévez, stood out. The inspector had written down the names of the musicians on a piece of paper: Arthur O'Neal and Iria Ledo. Yes, that ginger guy had to be O'Neal.

Nor did the solitary man with the shock of white hair seem to be from the village. Dressed in an immaculate dark suit, he kept a little apart from the rest. He stood with his head bowed and his face in his hands as the sunlight danced on his hair. The inspector had the impression the man was crying. Tears did not sit well with the spring sun.

Caldas thought he had seldom seen such a head of white hair. In most cases it is peppered with grey or yellow, but not in this one.

Rafael Estévez was waiting at the back. He'd sought the cool of the shade near the wall of the mausoleum. He whispered to Caldas to come and join him there.

'What is it?' Caldas whispered back.

'Read this tombstone, inspector.'

Caldas read the epitaph graven in marble: Here lies Andrés Lema Couto, who died on 23 July at sea, and whom the sea sent back to me for burial on 4 August 1981. Your grateful wife will always be with you.

'Is she thanking the sea for taking her husband?' asked Estévez.

'No, she's grateful because it gave him back.'

'But it gave him back dead,' replied Estévez in dismay.

'People who live by the sea know the risks, Rafa. They know one can die any day. The sense of unease is not caused by death, but by not having a body to bury. When a boat goes down and the drowned don't surface, their families remain on the shore mourning ghosts. This man's wife has her husband, even if he's here at the cemetery. The wives of the disappeared have no one. They turn into widows who look at the sea every day wondering about their loved ones. And so every day, without answers.'

'When you put it that way . . .'

Inspector Caldas went back to the other side of the mausoleum. The gravedigger had put down the trowel and climbed down the ladder, pleased at having done his bit in the funerary rite. The stone plaque would not come up for a few days yet, not until the stonemason delivered it, but the coffin had been put away and the mother could now leave.

But first everyone offered her their condolences. The children, standing in a line, stepped ahead one by one and kissed her. One of the little ones even managed to raise a fleeting smile on her face.

The policemen saw her go past as she was leaving, arm in arm with one of the townswomen, her face visibly distressed. Leo Caldas could relate to that pain which ate you from within. Hopefully she would never find out the precise circumstances of her son's death.

Caldas then looked around for the man with the white hair. He didn't see him. The man must have left as he and Estévez were talking about death and the sea. Only those he'd identified as musicians were in front of the tomb.

'What now, inspector?' asked Estévez.

'We'll wait outside,' replied the inspector as he lit a cigarette.

↬

And so they waited until the musicians started to leave. Once they were all out, Caldas took the piece of paper with their names out of his pocket, and approached the Irishman:

'Arthur O'Neal?'

The man replied in a thick foreign accent.

'That's me.'

'Could we have a word? It will only take a moment.'

Caldas took a drag on his cigarette, threw it on the floor and trod on it. He introduced himself as they stepped aside:

'I'm sorry to trouble you on a day like this, but it's important. My name's Inspector Caldas, from the Vigo police station, and I'd like to . . .'

'Caldas from the radio?' interrupted the musician.

'Yes, from the radio,' replied Caldas, without believing his ears: even the Irishman knew *Patrol on the Air*. 'I'd like to ask you when it would be convenient to speak to both of you, as Reigosa's band mates.'

'Just a moment.' O'Neal turned to the group. 'Iria, could you come over for a sec?'

The small woman's eyes were red from crying. The dark circles under her eyes contrasted with the white skin of her face.

Caldas excused himself once again for his bad timing, but she confirmed they were prepared to do anything that might help solve the murder of the saxophonist. They arranged to meet in Vigo. The musicians were giving a concert at the

Grial that night in tribute to Reigosa. It started at ten. They could talk in peace afterwards, at around eleven-thirty.

To Leo Caldas it seemed a nice gesture, bidding a final farewell to the dead man with music, rather than just mourning him.

'You know, the show must go on,' said Arhtur O'Neal with a sad expression by way of goodbye, as if he'd read his thoughts.

Dip

Although he hadn't been back since he was a child, Leo Caldas vividly remembered the trees planted on Lapamán beach. He recalled the soft, whiter-than-usual sand, and the beached boats known as *dornas*. The combined smell of sea, paint and the wood of the small fishing boats had remained nestled in his memory. Since then, the region had been invaded by an implacable bad taste, and he shuddered to think what the passage of time may have done to the place; but being close by, he decided to run the risk, and suggested to his assistant that they take a break at the beach.

They dropped away from the cemetery, and took a road parallel to the waterfront, which wound its way through a forest of pines and eucalyptuses. Rafael was driving slowly, as Caldas didn't quite remember where the turning was. They had barely covered two kilometres when a sign pointed the way. Caldas didn't really trust it, but it was right. The narrow path ended almost on the sand, in a parking space for only a few cars.

Once they'd parked, the officers walked down a stone staircase until they felt the crunching of the sand beneath their feet. The beach was deserted, except for a young woman sunbathing with her two small children, and another one picking seaweed along the shore.

There were two or three stone houses at the bottom of the beach which Leo didn't remember from his childhood, but they may have been there all along. No sign of the fishing boats, though.

They sat down beneath some trees, which were still standing by the sea as in Caldas's memory. The inspector grabbed a handful of sand and let it slip through his fingers. Just like before: white and fine.

'Some beach, inspector. And almost all to ourselves. This is paradise,' said Estévez looking around. 'Is it always like this?'

'Well... There are more people in the summer, but it's never an invasion.'

Used as he was to the Mediterranean, Estévez was amazed at the extension of beach that the low tide had uncovered. He took off his shoes and strolled over to the water's edge.

The inspector remained lying on the sand, with his eyes half-closed, mentally going over the case he had in his hands. He thought that if nothing came of the conversation with the jazz musicians that night, the formaldehyde was the best lead. Clinical formaldehyde may be in common use, but Barrio had mentioned that no one but a specialist was likely to know what the effects of injecting it would be. That pointed in the direction of pathologists and the clinical assistants in their departments. At least, thought Caldas optimistically, it wasn't a very popular profession. And although one couldn't go around prying into everyone's sexual preferences, homosexuals no longer hid in the closet. He had also the names of the hospitals that Freire had given him at Riofarma: the General Hospital, the Policlinic and the Zuriaga Foundation. Riofarma was an important provider even if it wasn't the only one, and he had to start somewhere. There was also Reigosa's car. Sooner or later it was bound to turn up.

The seaweed gatherer walked past the inspector. On her head she was balancing a full basket. Caldas stayed where he was, looking at the trees swaying over his head, with the breeze blowing on his face. To one side he could see the other woman playing with her two kids. He thought of Alba. He understood her desire to be a mother, but was hurt by the fact that she refused to acknowledge that having a child requires absolute conviction. You couldn't do it on a whim.

Besides, they had to be in complete agreement about decisions affecting them both. He'd once read that children were the main cause of tension between couples. It was obviously true, even if those children were only hypothetical.

'It's cold,' said Estévez, who'd come back from the shore with wet feet, 'but what with the heat and all, I'd feel as good as new if I went in for a dip. You don't mind if I go in my underpants, do you?'

'Me?' replied Caldas without looking up. 'So long as we're back in time for tonight's concert.'

Estévez peeled off his clothes in a flash and ran off, raising clouds of sand wherever he trod.

When Caldas sat up to shake himself, he saw the one hundred and thirty kilos of his assistant running in his underpants across the wide beaches of Lapamán. And as he went into the water, splashing about like a galloping horse, Caldas remembered the poisonous weaverfish.

Presently Estévez left the water cursing, and balancing on one leg. He was holding his other foot with both his hands.

Out of Tune

When Inspector Caldas came out of Eligio's, it had gone half past nine in the evening. The sun had already set, but it was still light.

Eligio's was an endangered species on account of its old smells of stone, wood and wisdom. But its best-kept secret was a small kitchen away from the visitor's eyes, where they cooked the tastiest octopus in the city. Caldas had had dinner at the bar, chatting with Carlos, while a group of university professors had a debate at the next table.

He'd gone for a small dish of beef stewed on a low heat, with potatoes seasoned with olive oil and a mixture of paprika and cayenne pepper, and a good portion of scallop quiche, served just the way he liked it: the pastry thin and crispy, and the scallops simply cooked with browned onions. Carlos had opened a bottle of white for both of them before dinner. One conversation had led to another one.

⁀

Caldas walked down Príncipe Street, across Puerta del Sol, and under an arch that had once been one of the two gates into the old city. He pressed on along the cobblestones, leaving behind the university library and the bishop's private residence on his right. He then took a little street in the direction of Santa María Church, and went into Gamboa Street. The Grial was at number five.

From outside it looked a bit like an English pub, with its strips of dark wood framing the small white façade. The door and window frames were as dark, and the windows had nice bevelled glass. At the entrance, a small slate gable jutted out over the pavement like a visor.

The Grial was comfortable inside, with a long bar to the

right and a dozen tables scattered over the remaining space. Nearly all were taken, mostly by groups of four or more people. Images of jazz grandees hung on the walls, and Cole Porter played through the loudspeakers.

Caldas approached the crowded bar. When his turn came, he asked for some wine, in order not to mix drinks. At the back he made out the low stage. The Irishman, sitting on a stool, was tuning his bass. Next to him was a black piano with a microphone poised at an angle to it.

As he looked around, Caldas spotted Iria Ledo at the bar, barely a couple of metres away. Even with make-up, she hadn't managed to conceal her dark circles. Leo lit a cigarette and approached her.

'Good evening.'

'Inspector Caldas, we were not expecting you until after the concert.'

'I though I might find good music here,' replied Caldas, as if justifying himself.

'There's been better nights,' said Iria Ledo.

'Of course. I'm sorry for your loss.'

Caldas fell silent as she acknowledged his comment with a nod.

'I guess it won't be easy to go on stage without Reigosa.'

'You can be sure of that, inspector.'

Iria took two glasses from the barman and changed the subject:

'Do you like jazz?'

Caldas nodded.

'I've never seen you round here before, though.'

'I'm a creature of habit,' the policeman excused himself. 'And I usually listen to music at home. I've only been here once.'

'You seem to have chosen the worst time for your second visit.'

Caldas knew this, but her words carried not so much a reproach as sincere sorrow.

'I'm all too aware of that,' he replied.

'Well, we'll talk later, inspector,' she said. 'We're about to start.'

Iria Ledo turned round and walked away between the tables with a glass in each hand. Once on stage, she passed Arthur O'Neal one of them, took a sip from the other, put it on the floor, and sat at the piano.

The background music stopped, and the lights were dimmed until the Grial was almost in darkness. A spotlight picked out Iria, pale at her black piano. She brought her fingers down on the keyboard with her eyes closed. Leo soon identified the piece: 'Embraceable you', by Gershwin. Bass notes and a slow rhythm. It had to be played with feeling, but Iria had feeling to burn.

Once it was over, and the applause died down, Iria finished her drink and grabbed the microphone. She told the audience that Luis Reigosa wouldn't be there that night, though Leo had the impression that most of the people at the bar already knew of his death. Then, in a sad voice, she explained that they would like to pay homage to him, apologised in advance for whatever blunders their emotions might hold in store, and introduced Arthur O'Neal on bass. The duo played several pieces Leo wasn't quite able to recognise. Perhaps, he thought, they were playing them just the way they did when Reigosa was with them, and he didn't recognise them because of the absence of the saxophone.

Later, a certain German Díaz came on stage with a local type of hurdy-gurdy called *zanfoña*. Caldas knew that some traditional Galician instruments were being introduced into jazz bands, but it was the first time he'd heard that kind of fusion and was pleasantly surprised. They played Charlie Parker's 'Laura', with the *zanfoña* standing in for the saxophone. The *zanfoña* didn't have the range of the sax and it wasn't easy to replace wind with cords, but the old instrument sounded as if it were crying. Not for Laura, as Parker's sax, but for Reigosa.

The show finished with a song that Iria dedicated especially to Luis Reigosa: 'Angel Eyes'.

Caldas had not forgotten the water-blue colour of the dead man's irises, and thought 'Angel Eyes' a perfect title for that tribute.

And why my angel eyes ain't here
Oh, where is my angel eyes.

And when, from his place at the bar, the inspector heard Iria's tearful voice singing, he knew there couldn't be a better farewell gift.

Excuse me while I disappear
Angel eyes, angel eyes.

After the performance, Iria Ledo and Arthur O'Neal sat down with Caldas at a table near the bar. They told him Reigosa was not only a good man, but also an excellent musician who lived for his saxophone. He spent his afternoons at the conservatory and his evenings here at the Grial.

They talked about generalities for a while until Caldas asked:

'Do you know if Reigosa was gay?'

'Of course,' replied Iria, and Caldas knew he was blushing slightly. 'We saw each other nearly every day. Luis never hid it. He wasn't a militant homosexual either, but if anyone asked he had no problem answering he was gay. Did you see his eyes?'

'His eyes?' The inspector had been unable to forget them from the moment he'd first seen them.

'Luis's,' clarified Iria, as if it were necessary. 'His eyes were a magnet for both men and women, he couldn't help it. Does it make any difference who he chose to sleep with?'

'He was killed in his bed,' explained Caldas.

'Oh, they hadn't told us.'

Arthur couldn't get his head round the possible reasons.

'Luis was a regular guy,' he said in his thick accent. 'He

never got into trouble with anyone, and no one had reason to do him any harm.'

'But they did.'

'We know. It was us that identified the body,' said Iria, visibly upset. 'His face showed he'd been in a lot of pain.'

Fortunately, they hadn't seen the rest of the body.

'So how come you identified the body?'

'The alternative was to let his mother do it,' replied the pianist. 'The poor woman. At the funeral I almost thought she'd go with him.'

O'Neal grimaced as he remembered the scene.

'Luis wanted to be cremated.'

'He spoke of his death?'

'We're musicians, inspector. We spent many nights in this bar, the three of us – Art, Luis and me. There are times when you drink, talk and imagine things. Just for the sake of it, you know. A wedding, a journey, a funeral... stuff. Once Luis said he wanted to be cremated and his ashes scattered on the sea with Bird... with Charlie Parker for soundtrack.'

Caldas nodded.

'Why didn't you carry out his wishes?'

'Would you have told that to his mother? Luis is... was her only child. He'd upset her enough by moving to Vigo. He'd grown up without a father, you know.'

The inspector knew exactly what she meant. In the Galician rural world, it was neither strange nor frowned upon that a woman of a certain age should bring up children alone. An old woman without offspring was pretty much doomed to mendicity if she couldn't work the land. So everyone understood that she may want to have a child who'd help her in the future. Even so, Reigosa had decided on other plans.

'Was he in a relationship?' asked Caldas, looking at the pale woman.

'Luis? Not that I know of.'

A bit hesitant, Iria turned to the Irishman, who confirmed this.

'Luis told us what he wanted us to know, and we didn't ask him any questions beyond that. There may have been someone he saw more often than he saw others, but if there had been someone really special we would have known. Don't you think, Art?'

Arthur nodded emphatically, and the light from the candle at the centre of the table played curiously on his reddish hair.

The woman went on:

'We knew that sometimes, after a concert, he'd go to a pub in the Arenal, but I can't remember its name. Art, do you know the one I mean?'

'The Idílico?'

'Yes, the Idílico, I'm pretty sure that's it. You may find something there, inspector, but I can't imagine Luis leading a double life. The one he had was quite enough.'

The Irishman, who in the course of the conversation had downed two enormous glasses of beer, excused himself and made for the toilet. Leo stayed with the woman, and got out another cigarette, which he lit from the flame of the candle.

'One more thing – I was surprised to see where Reigosa lived. Is there so much money in music?'

'So much, inspector? We all get by, more or less.'

'But what he got here and a supply teacher's salary at the conservatory doesn't seem enough to be able to live in a duplex in Toralla.'

'Luis wasn't worried about savings, inspector. He was not planning on starting a family – far from it.'

Certainly, Caldas thought, as the woman said:

'There's your friend.'

'Sorry?'

'The big guy at the door. Wasn't he with you at the funeral?'

Caldas saw Estévez limp towards the bar and lean on it.

'Good memory,' he said, nodding.

Before saying goodbye, he asked the pianist:

'Did you see a very elegant man at the cemetery? A white-haired man.'

'I did, and actually noticed the hair and the clothes. Very white hair, and a beautiful suit. Who was he?'

'I don't know.' Caldas lamented again that he hadn't seen his face. 'I meant to talk to him, but he was no longer there when we left. Would you mind asking O'Neal if he ever saw that man with Reigosa?'

'Of course, inspector.'

They stood up, and the light from a fluorescent tube tinged the pianist's pale skin blue. They shook hands.

'Many thanks, Iria, I'm sorry for disturbing you at time like this.'

She said he needed not apologise, and Caldas left her his card.

'If you think of anything else please give me a call. Sometimes the smallest things...'

She held the card in her hand, without looking at it.

'When was the other time?' she asked.

'What do you mean?'

'The other time you came to the Grial, that concert you mentioned. What was the occasion, inspector?'

'An American pianist... Bill Garner if I remember rightly. He was said to be Errol Garner's son. Do you know him?'

'Of course. Apollo.'

'Apollo?'

'That's his nickname,' the woman explained. 'I don't know who his father is. He sees himself as the new Thelonious Monk, but I don't think he's that good. For some things it's not enough to be black. I think he lives in Lisbon, so he pops round once or twice a year. He must have a girl here.'

'You don't seem to like him.'

'Apollo? I like him all right, but whenever he plays, my piano goes out of tune.' For the first time that night, the woman smiled. 'Please don't tell anyone, inspector.'

After the small woman took her leave, Leo Caldas watched

her make her way through the crowd. He stubbed out his cigarette in a nearby ashtray and made for the bar to join Estévez.

'Better late than never.'

'If we say after dinner, I come round after I have my dinner. Besides, I can barely walk, inspector. I had to lie down with my foot up from the moment I got home. My toes look like sausages thanks to that fucking piranha...'

'Weaverfish.'

'Weaverfish, that's right, the little son of a bitch. I'll never go into the sea again without a gun.'

Bluntness

After leaving the Grial, they took a good half-hour to walk four hundred yards. Estévez stopped at every bench along the Alameda Boulevard, complaining of his sore foot. At each stop he uttered a different curse.

Although it was a weekday, quite a lot of people had come to the pubs of Arenal Street. As he and his assistant picked their way through the crowd, Caldas remembered the caller who'd complained about the noise that stopped her sleeping at night. When you came to think of it, it was odd that he didn't receive more calls registering the same complaint.

It was a few minutes before one by the time they reached the Idílico, which was cordoned off with a rope in red velvet.

'Good evening,' said Leo.

A bouncer wearing a shirt and trousers with suspenders unhooked one of the ends of the cordon.

'Good evening.'

'But all that walking wasn't just to come and have a drink, was it, inspector?' complained Estévez, when he saw the place.

Caldas had twice tried to tell his assistant that they were heading for a gay bar where Reigosa was a regular, but Rafael interrupted him both times with his whingeing about the pain in his foot and the fish sting.

'What do you think?'

'What do I know?' Then Estévez added half to himself: 'I guessed a simple "yes" or "no" would be too much to ask for.'

'No,' spat Caldas, sick of his muttering.

They walked into the pub, which was dark and played electronica one decibel above what seemed bearable. Twelve or fifteen guys were on the dance floor, and a further five were propped against the bar.

Estévez went to take a seat in one of the armchairs near the dance floor. He pulled a table towards him and put his wounded foot on it, keeping it elevated. Leo asked him to wait and walked over to the bar. The barman's T-shirt looked as if it was about to burst.

'What can I get you?'

'What wines have you got?'

'Cheap wine, darling,' replied the barman in a camp voice.

'A beer, then,' said the inspector.

The guy with the tight T-shirt looked at Estévez:

'And for the big guy?'

'Another one.'

When the barman came back with the drinks, Leo got the photograph of Reigosa out of the pocket of his jacket. He placed it on the bar and turned it so that the barman could see it properly.

'Do you know this guy?'

'We don't know anyone here, it's company policy,' the young man snarled, without even pretending to look at the picture.

Caldas placed a fifty-euro note on top of the photo.

'That only pays for one of the beers,' added the other.

When the inspector placed another fifty on top, the barman recovered from his temporary fit of amnesia.

'The beers are my treat,' he said, stuffing the hundred euros into his jeans. 'They call him "Big eyes". He's a friend of Orestes.'

'Of whom?'

The guy pointed upstairs.

'Orestes.'

Caldas looked in the direction of the finger, above the dance floor. A glass box, hanging from the ceiling by thick steel cables, served as the DJ's booth. Inside, a very slender guy was working the decks. His disproportionately-sized headphones partially concealed his head of cropped hair.

For the boy's own good, Caldas hoped those headphones

were more comfortable than the ones he used at the radio station. He'd sometimes wondered if Santiago Losada's were as cumbersome as his. He had the feeling the presenter personally took care of leaving the hardest ones to him just to torment him.

Caldas grabbed the drinks and went over to join his assistant. Estévez, who still had his foot on the table, leaned over and said:

'Inspector, those two guys behind you at the bar are kissing.'

'Fine,' replied Caldas tersely.

'Don't get me wrong, chief, I've got nothing against them.' Absorbed as he was in his sore foot, he hadn't noticed that he was in a gay bar until now. 'People can sleep with whomever they want.'

'Just concentrate on your beer, and keep an eye on mine for a moment,' Caldas asked, leaving the glasses on the table by his assistant's injured foot. 'I'll be right back.'

The inspector walked across the bar, over to the ladder leading up to Orestes's booth. He disliked the idea of climbing up such a light metal structure, but there was no other way of attracting the DJ's attention. Once at the top he got out the photo of Reigosa and knocked on the glass. The deafening noise of the loudspeakers on both sides of the booth forced Caldas to knock harder; he was positively banging on the glass by the time the young man noticed he was there and opened the door.

'I'm working,' he shouted.

'Are you Orestes?'

The DJ nodded his shaven head, and the inspector showed him the photograph.

'No,' said Orestes with a smile, his lips near the inspector's ear. 'Big eyes hasn't come round for a few days. You'll have to settle for somebody else.'

Caldas wanted to waste no time.

'I need to have a word with you. I'm a cop.'

'You're what?' the man frowned, and his ample forehead creased with wrinkles.

Caldas showed his badge.

'Inspector Leo Caldas,' he shouted.

'From the radio?'

It couldn't be.

'Yes, from the radio. Can you turn this down a bit?' he asked, pointing to the booming loudspeakers.

'This is a bar, inspector, I'm supposed to play music.'

'Let's go somewhere else, then,' shouted Caldas.

'I'm working, inspector.'

Leo gestured with the five fingers of his right hand.

'I'll only keep you for five minutes.'

Orestes agreed to it with a nod, and the inspector climbed down the fragile ladder without looking below.

As he waited for the boy by the dance floor, he glanced at the spot where he'd left Estévez. He smiled when he discovered that his assistant had taken off his shoe and his sock, and was resting his bare foot on the table without any consideration for propriety.

When the DJ joined him, Caldas asked him if there was somewhere quiet they could talk. Orestes led him to a chaotic storeroom, whose door muffled the noise a bit.

'So what are you after, inspector? Please get straight to the point, I have to be back in the booth in two songs.'

Leo lit a cigarette, offered one to the shaven-headed boy, and showed him the photograph once again.

'He's a musician, he's called Luis,' said Orestes.

'Yes, I know, Luis Reigosa. What else do you know about him?'

'I don't know him that well, inspector. He's not really a regular and doesn't stay long when he comes here. We've talked a couple of times, but not much. I don't think he likes the atmosphere here a lot.'

'When did you last see him?' asked Caldas.

'To be honest, I haven't seen Big eyes for a while now. As

I said, he's not a regular, inspector. He comes and stays until he finds someone. And then he leaves, you know.'

'No, I don't.'

'If he gets lucky, he leaves early. He doesn't bide his time here.'

Hearing the roaring music behind the door of the store-room, Caldas wasn't surprised that Reigosa tried not to stay there longer than strictly necessary. It wasn't the first time the inspector had been at a gay bar, and like other times he had the impression that many of the crowd gathering there had very little in common except their sexual orientation.

'Did he have a boyfriend?'

'Big eyes? Not that I know of. Why the question in the past?'

'Because he'd dead,' said Caldas coldly.

'What?' Orestes seemed not to have understood his answer.

'Yesterday Big eyes, as you call him, turned up dead, tied to his bed. Murdered, in fact.' Caldas was purposefully blunt.

Orestes was visibly shocked by the news, and Caldas noticed how his lower lip trembled.

'Good God! Are you sure?' exclaimed the DJ.

'Absolutely sure. That's why I'm here. We think it's quite likely that he was killed by a lover. Perhaps you know some of them.'

Orestes rubbed his shaven head, as if brooding over his answer.

'I'm asking you whether you know any of Reigosa's lovers,' the policeman insisted.

The lad glanced at him with bleary eyes.

'You don't have lovers, inspector. You have a partner or you sleep around. A guy like Luis Reigosa had no trouble sleeping with whomever he liked. You can do the maths,' said Orestes, looking towards the door. 'Off the top of my head, I don't know... I've seen him talk to many people, but I'm not sure if they were just friends or not. I'd need to have a think. Couldn't we talk some other time? I really have to go back to my booth.'

'Tomorrow?'

Orestes uttered a timid 'Yes' and the inspector asked:

'Before lunch?'

'I finish here at seven in the morning, inspector.'

'What time can you make it?' Caldas tried to corner the boy.

'I don't know... better in the afternoon. Five o'clock?'

'All right. Here?'

'No, not here,' the lad replied quickly. 'Do you know the Mexico Hotel?'

'Near the station?'

The DJ nodded.

'There's a cafe on the ground floor. Shall we say there at five? I'm sorry not to be of more help right now,' apologised Orestes, and rushed out of the storeroom.

Leo threw his cigarette on the floor, trod on it and went after him.

'One more thing.' Caldas held him by the shoulders, so that the boy had to look him in the eyes when he spoke. 'Do you know if Reigosa has a friend with completely white hair?'

Orestes didn't answer.

'Very very white,' insisted the inspector.

'Very white... No, I don't know who that might be.' His lip was no longer trembling. 'I'm sorry, inspector, the song's about to end. I really must go back up now.'

Orestes hurried upstairs, and as Caldas saw him get in the booth he had the feeling that the boy was hiding something. Perhaps he hadn't lied – he hadn't sounded like someone who's lying – but Caldas was pretty sure he wasn't telling the whole truth either. He'd been too shocked by the news of the musician's death, and Caldas could only think of two reasons for that reaction: either Reigosa wasn't just an acquaintance, or the shaven-headed boy was afraid of something. Perhaps it was a combination of both. In the circumstances, it might be in Caldas's best interest to meet him the following day. One could remember a lot of things during a sleepless night. There was also the risk that the boy might bolt.

Caldas went to join his assistant and claim his beer. It was then that he saw the commotion at the back of the room, in the middle of which stood Estévez, towering half a foot above everyone else. He was holding his gun in one hand and his shoe in the other, and was roaring with rage, completely wild. The volume of the music and the general hullabaloo meant Caldas had to approach the scene before he could make out his assistant's words:

'Whoever comes closer than two metres is a dead man.'

The policemen lost themselves in the hustle and bustle of Arenal Street.

'I thought you were tolerant of gay people?'

'I don't mind what people are,' replied Estévez, who, grinding his teeth, limped along with his eyes fixed on the ground. 'So long as they don't try to give me a foot massage!'

'Did you see his face after that caress of yours?' Caldas told him off.

'Well he can go fuck himself,' replied Estévez, without the least sign of remorse.

'Rafa, this can't go on. Is there not a way you can control yourself?'

'If I hadn't controlled myself I would have shot him.'

'It was bad enough with the beating,' said Caldas, picturing the state of the poor man's face.

'Don't play with me, chief. He was lucky my foot hurt so much, or else . . .' Estévez came to a halt in the middle of the pavement. 'Now, are you going to explain what we were doing in that dive? Don't tell me it was just for an arsehole to try and massage my foot.'

'Luis Reigosa was gay,' replied the inspector. 'He sometimes went to that bar too.'

'So I was right! The sax wasn't the only thing he liked blowing!'

'We'd better call it a night, Rafa. I'll tell you more tomorrow.'

Leo Caldas got home at around quarter past two. He lay down and, with his eyes fixed on the ceiling, unsuccessfully tried to fathom that nagging feeling which, since the day before, reminded him that he had missed something during the inspection of Reigosa's flat.

But as he fell asleep he forgot all about it.

He dreamed of pale hands and piano keys.

Legend

'You want me to draw up a list of all the people who have access to formaldehyde?' asked Ana Solla, chief of pathology at the General Hospital.

'If it's possible.'

'Inspector, this is not morphine we're talking about. Formaldehyde is not a product that requires any safety guidelines. It's not subject to any security measures. We don't even keep it in a locked place.'

'But isn't it highly toxic?' insisted Leo.

'Do you keep bleach at home under lock and key, inspector? This is a hospital, and the products are supposed to be handled by qualified staff. We have to be practical. If we had to fill in a form every time we need to use a product like formaldehyde, we'd spend our day writing instead of practising medicine, which is what we're here for.'

'So anyone could come and take it without leaving their details.'

'That's right. We ask no questions.'

'You must be the only ones around who don't,' muttered Estévez, who was behind the inspector.

'Could you tell me about the men in your medical staff, doctor?' asked Leo Caldas, trying another line of approach.

'Tell you about them?'

Caldas knew it was forbidden to smoke inside the hospital, but he instinctively reached for the packet of cigarettes he carried in his pocket. Alba used to tell him off for his habit of lighting up the moment he started a conversation: for hiding behind a shield of smoke.

'Yes, above all I'm interested in doctors, nurses, anyone

who might have access to formaldehyde and knows how it works.'

'How do you mean someone who "knows how it works"?' The doctor gave him a scornful look. 'Do you know what formaldehyde is, inspector?'

'Vaguely,' admitted Caldas, holding on to the cigarettes inside his pocket.

'We're talking about a preservative agent, whose use does not require any advanced medical knowledge.' The doctor grabbed a jar from a nearby table to accompany her explanation. 'You pour the solution, which you don't have to prepare because they send it already prepared from the lab, into a jar like this one,' she said, holding it up, 'and then you put in the tissue you want to preserve. The tissue is preserved without any further need for handling it. Do you think you'd need to know a lot about the product to be able to repeat that procedure?'

Caldas didn't reply. He was irritated by the doctor's manner. As a child he'd had to put up with a teacher who, instead of explaining to his pupils what they didn't know, made fun of their ignorance in front of the class. He asked the children to repeat their wrong answers out loud, and laughed at them, revealing a line of yellow teeth. The doctor's tone reminded Caldas of the inflexions the old teacher preferred.

'Are you sure you know what you're after, inspector?' asked the doctor again. 'I don't get that impression.'

'No, I'm not sure of anything, doctor. But I've got a crime on my hands for which a solution of thirty-seven per cent formaldehyde, just like the one you keep here, was used to murder the victim.'

'Formaldehyde poisoning?'

'Something like that,' replied Caldas with the feeling that the doctor, as his teacher had, was about to ask him to repeat it out loud.

'Could you tell me what you expect me to say?'

'We are convinced that the murderer had a certain knowledge of the toxicity of formaldehyde, as otherwise it would have been quite difficult for them to use it as a weapon.'

'Are you accusing me, inspector?'

Caldas shook his head.

'We believe the killer might be a man. We're looking for those men who match the profile.'

'And you expect me to tell you what the men I work with are like, just in case any of them matches the profile?'

Caldas found that mocking tone exasperating, and he had to control himself not to shout at her.

'Precisely, doctor,' he said, trying hard to look calm, 'that is indeed what we expect.'

The doctor thought it over for a few seconds.

'You only want the men's names, right?'

'For now,' confirmed Caldas.

'There's only one doctor here – Doctor Alonso.'

'And the assistants?' asked Caldas.

'Male assistants?' The chief doctor gave a contemptuous snort. 'None. And the nurses are all female too. There are no patients who need to be lifted here. We need more brains than brawn.'

Caldas was not there to listen to sarcastic remarks; he had enough of that kind of thing at the radio station.

'Is Doctor Alonso married?'

'I think so.'

'Any children?'

'Inspector, you're entering into personal matters. Those are questions that affect Doctor Alonso's privacy,' she complained.

Caldas bit his tongue not to reply that the question he'd really like to put to her was of a far more personal nature: whether she could tell him anything about her colleague's sexual orientation.

Instead he said: 'I'd like to cross him off my list without calling him in for an interrogation, doctor. As you can imagine, it wouldn't be pleasant for Doctor Alonso, or this department, or this hospital to become involved in a murder investigation. The press can be a real pest when there's a certain kind of scandal in the air.'

'Doctor Alonso has three or four children,' replied the doctor dryly. 'I'm not too sure. We can ask his secretary, if you like,' she said, gesturing in the general direction of the phone.

'I'd rather speak to him in person,' replied Caldas.

'I'm afraid that's impossible. Doctor Alonso is at a conference in the Canary Islands.'

'How long has he been away?'

'Does that matter?'

It did. The doctor grudgingly searched through the drawers of her desk until she found a year planner.

'The conference started on the seventh,' she read, placing it on the desk. 'The doctor left the previous day, if I remember correctly.'

That ruled out Doctor Alonso, as he was several hours away by plane at the moment of the crime.

'You can come by next Wednesday or Thursday, inspector. The doctor will be back by then.'

'It won't be necessary.'

Leo Caldas and Rafael Estévez stood up to leave.

'One last thing, doctor,' said Caldas. 'Are there any other areas where formaldehyde is used?'

She looked at him once again like his yellow-toothed teacher.

'Of course, inspector. It's used in operating theatres. They need to preserve tissue during many procedures, for example in biopsies, to name a simple one that you can understand. However, as I've already explained, we're not talking about cyanide. Anyone who may need formaldehyde, be it a doctor, a nurse or a laboratory assistant, can come along and take any quantity they need without giving any explanation.'

14 May felt autumnal from the moment the sun rose. A cloak of fog had come in from the mouth of the *ría* during the night, and it threatened to linger well into the morning.

After their visit to the General Hospital, the two policemen went over to the Policlinic in their search for suspects, where they met with similar success. The attending who received them could not think of someone familiar with formaldehyde who matched the characteristics that Caldas secretly attributed to Luis Reigosa's murderer. As for the list of male staff working in operating theatres, it comprised upward of two hundred and fifty people in those two hospitals alone. At least for now, Caldas decided to focus on the pathology departments, where the real experts worked. As Guzmán Barrio had said in the autopsy room, one needed quite a bit of specialised knowledge to inject formaldehyde into someone's genitals.

From the list Isidro Freire had given them, they still had to visit the Zuriaga Foundation, but Caldas wasn't expecting much there either. He was beginning to realise that the health sector was a close order, a far cry from those areas where malicious gossip is an everyday thing. No doubt the recent barrage of lawsuits filed against hospitals for negligence had forced health professionals to watch over each other's backs. It wasn't that odd; something similar was happening in the police force.

They got into the car and Caldas told his assistant to head for the Zuriaga Foundation on Monte del Castro.

'That's the hill up there, right?'

Caldas confirmed this was so.

'We have to go up in the direction of the park. After that, I'll guide you.'

Monte Castro was an elevation that dropped all the way to the sea. At the top were a castle and a park with a belvedere. The panoramic view of the city and its *ría* was a must on the tourist circuit, and the guides told legends of naval battles and sunken treasures. The Castro owed its name to an important archaeological discovery made many years ago in the area. In the first century AD, the Celts had built a fort or *castrum*, taking advantage of the drop and the unevenness of the terrain for their protection. They had never understood, those Celts, that a town could be built on those steep hill-sides. Many centuries later, the new inhabitants still questioned the idea, but in any case Vigo had been erected precisely on these hills.

‿

Caldas approached the service desk. The spacious lobby blended glass and granite, as did the other five storeys of the building. The Zuriaga maternity clinic, a small concern founded seven decades ago, had been successively renovated until it had become the most important private hospital in the city. It still delivered the children of the best families in Vigo, but several years ago it had also become a Foundation with many other interests. On its welcome sign, Caldas counted sixteen medical specialisms.

The second of these, in alphabetical order, was anatomo-pathology. The inspector asked after the head of the department.

'The head doctor is a woman,' specified the receptionist, and gave him her name. Then, pointing to the lifts: 'Third floor.'

Third floor and third woman, thought Caldas, hoping that this one would treat him better than the one at the General Hospital.

She listened to him attentively before she spoke.

'We do indeed work with formaldehyde. We store it in the next room. Please come with me.'

The doctor showed them a few boxes stacked up in a room adjoining her office. Caldas could see that the Zuriaga Foundation didn't have any security measures in place for it either.

'Most of it is used in our department. The rest in operating theatres.'

'Of course, for biopsies.' Caldas didn't need another lecture. 'Are there any men in your department? Any doctors or nurses?'

'No, we're two women doctors and three female nurses.'

'I should have thought so,' said Caldas tersely, resigning himself to getting only a register of the staff who worked in the operating theatre. He'd been hoping for a male specialist, a homosexual one if possible, to materialise right there and then, but he was reconciling himself to the idea that he'd have to work on a list of hundreds of names.

'Could you point me in the direction of management?' he asked, in order to get that list and leave as soon as possible.

~

Inspector Caldas and Officer Estévez walked into the top-floor offices. Through the glass wall they could see the westernmost side of the *ría*, which was still enveloped in fog. Had it not been for the fog, Caldas thought, they might have seen the twenty floors of the Toralla tower.

Across from the lifts, on the granite wall, hung a huge oil portrait of an old man with white hair and a prominent nose. His name was on the bottom of the canvas, along with a date and an inscription: 'Happiness lies in health, Gonzalo Zuriaga, 1976'.

They asked the girl at the desk for the list of surgeons, nurses and assistants, personal information included.

'I'll have to check,' she said. 'Just a moment.'

The girl withdrew to a back room to make a call. There were a dozen people working in the other offices, but no one else in the management area.

Estévez asked his boss what they were going to do once they had the list of staff who had access to operating theatres:

'What do you have in mind, inspector – call in the quacks one by one and check which team they play for?'

'I thought of locking them up with you and arresting whoever offers to give you a foot massage.'

'I'm being serious, inspector.'

'Have you got a better idea?'

The girl, who'd left her headset on the table, came back with an answer.

'Would you mind showing me your ID?'

'Of course, I'm Inspector Caldas,' he said, showing his badge.

'Inspector Caldas? Are you the one from the radio?'

'Yes, from the radio,' his confirmation sounded like a lamentation. 'And this is Officer Rafael Estévez.'

'You'll see how it's all plain sailing from now on,' whispered Estévez when the young woman went to relay the information to her interlocutor at the other end of the line.

'Sure,' replied Caldas.

When the girl returned, she looked more relaxed.

'Doctor Zuriaga asked me to make anything you might need available to you,' she announced. 'He also says he's sorry for not being able to see you in person, Inspector Caldas, but he hasn't been well the last couple of days and is resting at home. If I understood correctly, you'd like a list of all the staff with access to the operating room, is that right?'

Estévez smiled as he saw the turn the inquiry was taking once the girl had learned the identity of his superior.

'Would that be possible?' asked Leo Caldas.

'Is it OK if I print out the list of all the doctors and I point out the surgeons?'

'That would be perfect,' confirmed the inspector, 'but we also need a list of the nurses and any assistant that may have access to the operating rooms.'

'Only the male staff,' qualified Estévez.

The girl took a seat at a nearby computer.

'The system doesn't distinguish gender,' she explained. 'I think we'd better print the whole thing and then mark the men.'

She then pressed a key, and a dot-matrix printer loaded the first page at the other end of the office.

'It's a pleasure to find people as kind as you,' added Rafael Estévez winking at the girl, who smiled and stood up to go and collect the printout.

Caldas found it difficult to recognise his assistant in this flatterer with the beaming smile. He'd thought Estévez's inclination to barbaric acts would have kept him away from the roads to love.

'Rafa, are you flirting?' he asked in a low voice.

Estévez spoke into his superior's ear.

'Now I know why you became inspector so fast,' he whispered, 'you're a real Sherlock.'

Caldas didn't reply. He deserved Estévez's mocking answer.

The girl came back with the printout and a highlighter.

'Here's the list. We are all on it, from the first to the last in alphabetical order. This is me, see?' she announced happily, placing the highlighter on the page. 'But I'm afraid I'm not a man.'

Next to the fluorescent yellow dot, the policemen read: 'Diana Alonso Zuriaga. It couldn't be a coincidence.'

'Are you related?' asked the inspector, looking at the enormous painting on the wall.

'He was my grandfather on my mother's side,' she replied.

'You're lucky not to have his nose,' joked Estévez.

'It was a close brush,' said Diana cheerfully. 'The nose passed down to my uncle Dimas.'

'Dimas Zuriaga?' asked Caldas, who'd heard that name on many occasions.

'Yes,' she answered, 'Doctor Zuriaga is my uncle. He inherited grandfather's nose, and his hair.'

And his clinic, thought Caldas while looking at the painting. Old man Zuriaga's hair was as white as the dressing gown in which he had sat for the painting. The inspector, for the first time in two days, had the feeling he was on the right track.

Estévez joked again about hereditary traits and the girl

laughed heartily. Caldas couldn't remember the last time one of his comments had made a woman burst out laughing.

'If you like I'll start underlining the names of the people who have access to the operating theatres,' she offered, waving the highlighter around.

'Yes please,' agreed Caldas, flicking to the last page. 'But just let me see one thing.' The name he was looking for was on it. He gave the printout back to the girl.

Sense

The noonday sun, quickly dispelling the fog, heralded another hot summer day. At the *ría*, through the remaining mist, one could make out the flat-bottomed boats lined up like a fleet of ghost ships.

Inspector Caldas was sunk in the passenger seat with his eyes closed. The shrill ring of his mobile brought him back to reality.

'Two things – is that animal you call your assistant there with you?' asked Superintendent Soto at the other end of the line. He didn't sound too cheerful.

'Yes,' answered Caldas dryly.

'Do you know what he did last night?'

Caldas would rather the superintendent told him.

'Last night?'

'Leo, don't beat about the bush. If you know, just own up.'

'No idea, sir.'

'It seems he went out hunting.'

'Hunting?' asked Caldas, as if he hadn't understood.

'Hunting. Your assistant went to a gay bar on Arenal, sat in provocative poses, and kicked the first guy who went near him. Apparently, he kicked him so bad that he hurt his foot, because soon enough he had taken off his shoe and was bashing him in the face with its heel. He's a complete lunatic. It seems that, meanwhile, he threatened people with his gun, so no one dared approach as he finished the job.'

As always when they talked about Estévez, there was an element of truth and a lot of fantasy.

'A couple of lawyers from one of those poncey firms left my office only a half-hour ago,' went on Superintendent

Soto agitatedly. 'They want to file a lawsuit for injuries. Today.'

'I can't make head nor tail of what you're telling me. Couldn't they have mistaken him for someone else? Perhaps it wasn't him.'

'I don't care if it was him or not,' roared Soto through the receiver. 'Estévez is a barbarian. He's clocked up fourteen complaints in only a few months. Do you think that's normal?' Caldas tactfully fell silent, and the superintendent went on yelling. 'Well I don't, Leo. We're the police force, have you not read what it says on your badge? The police, the good guys, the guys who go after the bad guys. We're in charge of keeping public order. That's what they pay us for, not to let seven-feet tall aggressive psychopaths out on the loose, armed with handcuffs and a regulation gun. What the hell's the matter with you? Can't you at least control him?'

Caldas thought it wasn't the moment to explain he couldn't.

'Are you sure of what you say, sir? I was with Rafael all night and I didn't see him attack anyone. But since he's here I'll ask him. Just a moment.' He moved the mouthpiece away and addressed his assistant: 'Rafa, were you at a gay bar yesterday beating anyone up?'

Estévez looked at him in consternation, and Caldas had to point to the road for the car not to end in a ditch.

'He says "no", sir. I think on this occasion it's a mistake.'

'Leo, I do hope, for the good of us all, that you know nothing about this.' The superintendent took a moment to calm down. 'The other reason I was calling is that Reigosa's car has turned up.'

'Where?' asked Caldas. He hated his superior's habit of telling him the good news last.

'On a hill, on the other side of the *ría.*'

'Is forensics there?'

'Yes, I've already sent Ferro over, though I'm not sure it'll be worth it. They set fire to the car before abandoning it and it's completely burned out. If I'm not mistaken, you can kiss that line of inquiry goodbye.'

'One less,' muttered Caldas before ringing off.

The house was surrounded by a stone wall, the thick branches of a hundred-year-old yew tree jutting out. Estévez parked the car at the entrance. Leo got out, rang the bell and announced himself to the maid. He had to insist, saying he'd only take a few minutes of the doctor's precious time.

The huge mechanical gate slid open, revealing a paved driveway. Once inside, the car was flanked by the kinds of trees which had covered the Galician hills before the invasion of the eucalyptus: yew and pine trees, strong oaks, haughty birches, two enormous chestnut trees with twisted trunks, and the odd weeping willow.

A bit further down, the driveway took the shape of a circle, which went all the way up to the front door, so that vehicles could approach the foot of the stately steps anti-clockwise and carry on in the same direction on their way out. By the side of the road were camellia shrubs and rhodo-dendrons, which gave plenty of flowers all year round. Caldas remembered seeing an entrance like this one, even if considerably larger, at a castle he had once visited with Alba on a trip to the Loire valley.

The maid, dressed in a cap and apron, waited at the door, and asked them to follow her to the back of the house. They walked past a number of open windows, which aired an enormous dining room and a library with wood-panelled walls crammed with books. They also caught a glance of the imposing stone staircase leading up to the top floor.

The doctor's employee led them to a back porch.

'You may wait here,' she said tersely, pointing to some wicker chairs around a rustic table under the porch. Its slate roof was overhung with voluptuous purple bougainvillea flowers.

In contrast with the forest at the front of the house, a

thick blanket of grass extended before them, a green peninsula jutting into the *ría*. The yard ended in rocks on all sides, and the sea whipped up its white foam against them. A sailboat was moored to a stone quay protected by a breakwater. A path cut across the grass slope like a scar, passing by an old pond turned into a pool, and descending through the azaleas to the quay. Caldas reckoned the property's waterfront must be nearly a kilometre wide.

According to an old Galician proverb, '*If it has a chapel, a dovecot and a cypress, it really is an ancestral home.*' Caldas didn't know whether or not Zuriaga's place housed either of the first two, but it had plenty of nobility.

'Nice gaff they've got here!' exclaimed Estévez when the maid had left them. 'Who is this guy anyway, a maharajah?'

'In a way,' replied Caldas.

Although he hadn't reached the title of maharajah, Doctor Zuriaga was an important personage, and the Foundation he directed was hardly your run-of-the-mill health institute.

Dimas Zuriaga's father, Don Gonzalo Zuriaga, had devoted a room on the ground floor of his maternity clinic to his collection of Galician painting. Following in his footsteps, the son had channelled some of the Foundation's funds towards the sponsorship of the arts, until it became the main cultural driving force in the city. In its modern exhibition salon, which housed the permanent collection in the centre of Vigo, one could find most of the avant-garde figures of European art. The special exhibitions were often mentioned in the Sunday papers and the culture supplements of the broadsheets, which gave the Foundation an air of distinction. Artistic patronage aside, the fame of the Zuriaga Foundation as a health centre kept growing, and in the last few years it had seen a boost in revenues.

Doctor Zuriaga watched over all these activities. He'd given up his work as a surgeon quite some time ago in order to devote himself entirely to the management of the institution.

He had turned the small maternity clinic into one of the economic and cultural engines of Galicia, but he did not give interviews and refused to make public appearances. Called to explain his reluctance to take centre stage, he claimed the Zuriaga Foundation was not the fruit of his personal work but the responsibility of a whole team.

Some years back, the doctor's uncommon desire for privacy had produced the opposite effect in the press, and allusions and speculations on his slippery personality had naturally proliferated. In time, however, the media had ended up getting used to the fact, and at present it was only very seldom that they alluded to it.

'You still haven't told me what we're doing here, chief,' commented Estévez looking at his superior.

'I haven't, no.'

Leo Caldas sat quietly in one of the chairs under the porch. He didn't have an answer for his assistant, not a solid enough one anyway. He could have said that they were paying Zuriaga a visit because he had white hair, or tried to explain he'd had a strange feeling when he'd seen the portrait of old Gonzalo Zuriaga. He might have added that Zuriaga had been away from the Foundation for two days, which coincided with the time that had passed since the murder of Luis Reigosa; he might have commented he didn't believe in coincidences. But the inspector kept silent.

He knew these lines of reasoning were based on very little, and didn't need Estévez to remind him with his usual bluntness. Come to think of it, he didn't even have a reason to go after a man with white hair. The only real justification for it was that the play of sunlight on that person's head had attracted his attention at the cemetery, and that the musicians were unable to tell him who he was. That was all, and it wasn't much.

To make matters worse, he hadn't seen the man's face, which made it very unlikely, not to say impossible, that he should recognise him if he saw him ever again. True, the hair was exceptionally white, but there must be hundreds of white-haired men in the city, and it wasn't an unheard-of coincidence to come across someone with that kind of hair at one of the hospitals they had visited. Quite possibly he had crossed other men in that category who had not attracted his attention. And he didn't need to pay Doctor Zuriaga a visit to confirm that age had given him a hoary head. His niece had confirmed this without Caldas's even asking.

Besides, even if Dimas Zuriaga did turn out to be the man from the cemetery, the only reasonable conclusion was that he knew Reigosa. But many people did, and that didn't make them all suspects.

So the inspector was well aware that he hadn't looked hard enough into all this and that the visit might prove premature. He hadn't even talked to Reigosa's mother or his colleagues at the conservatory where he had taught as a supply teacher. The man with the unusual hair might be a relative, a childhood friend or co-worker. He might even be the saxophone teacher the musician was temporarily replacing.

In addition, Caldas knew he wouldn't get much from a conversation with the doctor, and that a slip vis-à-vis such an important man might entail irreversible consequences. Zuriaga moved in social circles where the sexual aspects of the case would prove scandalous, and the gutter press would not be slow to divulge such a thing. Even so, he decided to go ahead and follow his hunch, which hardly ever failed him, although he made it a point to act with the supreme caution that someone like Zuriaga required and deserved.

So he hadn't had time to slip up – not yet.

Excuse

Sitting in the shade under the back porch of the doctor's imposing house, Leo Caldas and Rafael Estévez awaited Dimas Zuriaga. Estévez, panting, said that that morning, when he had looked out of the window to see what clothes he should wear, he had only seen grey mist. Now at noon, the May sun shone on his corduroy shirt, and he was boiling.

The inspector was looking at the photograph of Luis Reigosa when an elegantly dressed woman came out of the house through a sliding door.

'Good afternoon,' she greeted them.

As if a colonel had turned up in front of two recruits, both policemen stood to attention, and Caldas returned the picture to his pocket.

'Good afternoon,' they said back.

'Please, don't get up,' said the woman, matching her words with a soft gesture of her hand. 'They've told me you've come to see my husband. Would you like anything to drink while you wait? Knowing him, it wouldn't surprise me if he takes his time to come down.'

'Well...' Estévez's imploring eyes sought his boss. To no avail.

'We're fine,' stammered Caldas, who was a bit surprised that Dimas Zuriaga was married to such a woman.

'I'm Mercedes Zuriaga,' she said, offering her hand.

Caldas shook her long fingers gently.

Before his turn, Estévez wiped his sweaty palm on the leg of his trousers.

Mercedes Zuriaga was tall and slender. She was wearing a cream dress with a belt that hugged her waist. Her décolletage exposed her collarbones, and she had a long elegant neck.

Her dark hair was tightly combed back and tied into a pony-tail. The inspector guessed she must be in her late forties, but whatever her age she was still very attractive. Perhaps even more attractive than she had been as a young woman.

'Do sit down, please,' she said, and the policemen obeyed even though she remained standing.

'You referred to yourself as inspector. Are you policemen?'

Leo's awkward frown confirmed it; he knew that police visits had the same terrible reputation as that of the albatross on a boat at sea.

'Has anything happened?' asked Mrs Zuriaga anxiously.

'No, nothing to worry about,' said Caldas reassuringly. 'We'd only like a word with your husband. We were at the Foundation, and as we missed him there we took the liberty of coming over.'

The woman nodded with an oscillation of her heron's neck, and the inspector went on:

'Your niece already told us that Doctor Zuriaga...'

'My niece?'

'Isn't the girl who works at the management office a niece of yours?'

'Oh, Diana, of course.'

'That's right, Diana,' confirmed the inspector. 'We saw her this morning. She'd warned us that Doctor Zuriaga was a bit unwell. I hope it's nothing serious – we wouldn't want to trouble you.'

'Don't worry, inspector. These days my husband says he's ill, but I don't think he's got anything, really.' Mercedes Zuriaga gave him a slightly conspiratorial smile. 'It's often just an excuse to work from home, without phones ringing or people interrupting him.'

Caldas took this in a spirit of sportsmanship.

'I'm not surprised he prefers to stay in. You have a beautiful house.'

'Yes, that's true,' replied Mercedes Zuriaga looking at the garden that dropped off into the sea. 'Quite beautiful.'

When Leo Caldas finally saw the doctor he was slightly disappointed. He'd been expecting an inner voice confirming Zuriaga was the person he had noticed at the cemetery, but no such revelation occurred. Although he knew that its absence proved neither one thing nor the other, it was a small drawback for someone who trusted his instinct.

Dimas Zuriaga was wearing a loose white shirt, which he hadn't tucked into his blue trousers. His dark-rimmed tortoiseshell glasses were hanging on his chest by a brown piece of cord. His nose was large, and his hair white. Very white.

He approached the porch and, after greeting them politely, asked in a deep voice:

'Haven't they offered you anything to drink?'

'They have, thank you. Your wife insisted, but there's no need.' Caldas looked around for the doctor's wife, but she had withdrawn as silently as she had appeared, leaving the three men on their own. 'We won't be long.'

Dimas Zuriaga sat down, and the policemen did likewise.

'They called me from the Foundation to inform me of your visit. I expect they treated you well,' he said, and Caldas nodded. 'I would have seen you myself, but as you no doubt know, my health is not at its best these days. I hope you'll excuse me.'

'Of course, doctor. They've told us you haven't left the house for a few days. Are you feeling better?'

'Well, no worse than usual,' he replied.

He obviously didn't understand the reason that had brought the policemen to his home address, so he added:

'I gather that they gave all the information you were looking for at the Foundation. Is that so, inspector?'

'Indeed, your niece was very kind,' replied Caldas laconically.

Dimas Zuriaga waited a few seconds for another answer that might explain the presence of the policemen there, but was greeted with silence.

'Is anyone going to tell me the reason for this visit?'

Estévez, as eager for an answer as his host, fidgeted in his seat, making its wicker creak unpleasantly. Caldas decided to get straight to the point and show Zuriaga the picture of Reigosa. He slid it on the table, as a croupier would a card, in the direction of the doctor.

'Do you happen to know this man?'

Estévez's chair creaked again when Zuriaga took the photograph. The doctor put his glasses on his protruding nose, screwed up his eyes and, after a few seconds, shook his head.

'I don't know him,' he said, returning the picture to Caldas.

'Are you sure, doctor? Perhaps you've bumped into him at an official occasion hosted by the Foundation...' insisted Caldas.

'Completely sure. I don't deal with many people, inspector. So I hardly ever forget a face.'

The instinct that had failed to materialise when Doctor Zuriaga appeared suddenly sprung up in Caldas: it told him that Zuriaga was not telling the truth. Almost without thinking, he took a chance.

'How do you explain that we have a witness who's prepared to testify that you and this man knew each other?' he lied.

'I don't know, you tell me,' replied the doctor, in the scandalised voice of someone unused to being contradicted.

Leo Caldas hesitated, but once on the offensive he couldn't beat a retreat. He doubted he'd ever have another chance to confront the eminent man face to face. Stepping down would mean letting him get away.

'Were you at a funeral yesterday, Doctor Zuriaga?'

'I've already told you that yesterday, like the day before and today, I was indisposed,' replied the doctor without batting an eyelid. 'Do you understand, or would you rather my lawyer explained it to you, inspector?'

The car was making its way towards the exit among the hundred-year-old trees of the Zuriaga residence.

'What the hell was that all about? You can't think Zuriaga is involved in this? We're talking about a murder. And what was all that about the witness? Could you explain that, chief? You know as well as I do how powerful that man is. He can crush us just by picking up the phone. Besides, hadn't we agreed our man is gay? Doctor Zuriaga has a willowy brunette for a wife, inspector, you saw her as well as I did. Do you think anyone can be gay with a lady like that at home? Really, chief, I don't know what went through your head, but we'll get a right bollocking for this.'

Caldas remained silent, sunk in the passenger seat with his eyes closed. He had gambled – and he had lost.

Rafael Estévez wound down the car's window.

'Bloody hell it's hot!'

Absence

He had remembered his lunch engagement at the last possible moment. He was now hurrying down Arenal Street – and he was late. A few seconds later he pushed a glass door and rushed into the restaurant, his eyes darting from table to table. Once he found the right one, he went over and sat down in front of an older man who smiled at him.

'Leo!'

'I'm sorry I'm late, Dad.'

'Oh, don't worry about it,' his father said and then whispered, 'but you asked me to meet you at a place where they don't have my wine, and that is unforgivable.'

'What do you mean they don't have it? I always ask for it when I come here.'

'Well, today they don't have it,' his father insisted.

Caldas didn't want to add wine to his long list of problems.

'Excuse me, Cristina!' he called out.

The waitress approached the table.

'Hi, Leo, how's it going?'

'All right, I suppose. But my old man here is a bit disappointed, as he thinks you don't have his wine. I told him I always drink it, but ...'

'I'm afraid we had until a few days ago, when we sold our last bottles. Now we're waiting for the distributor to bring us some more.'

'You see, they usually have it,' said Caldas to his father, who didn't seem too pleased anyway.

'But today they don't.'

'If you like I can bring you any other one. They're not as delicious, but they're not bad either. I can offer you a variety of labels or the house wine,' explained the waitress, handling the situation with aplomb.

'Which one's better?' asked Caldas's father.

'There's no chemistry involved in the house wine,' she started explaining.

'Of course there's chemistry involved,' interrupted the old man. 'Or what do you think fermentation is? There's chemistry in everything, my girl. What that house wine of yours lacks is controlled fermentation, or bacteria filters, or proper stationing in casks, and many other things which are needed for a good wine as much as grapes. But chemistry . . .'

'So which one will it be?'

'Oh, well,' said the older man theatrically. 'The house wine.'

'And to eat?' asked Cristina.

'I'm in charge of oenological matters,' replied the father, raising the palms of his hands and waving towards Leo, as if fanning the air between them. 'The rest I leave to my son.'

As a starter Leo Caldas ordered half a kilo of goose barnacles which he had reserved over the phone, and as a main course a huge sole he chose from the display counter. He requested that it be boned after frying, so that he and his father could share it more easily.

At these restaurants in the harbour you had to eat on a paper tablecloth, amid much noise, and sometimes even sharing a table; but they had fish and seafood fresh from the generous Galician *rías*, instead of the bland ones trucked over from distant seas, as in other restaurants. 'How can you ask for goose barnacles, darling? Haven't you seen the sea today?' Cristina had scolded a few times when, in spite of the bad weather, he asked for his favourite dish. The food was *that* fresh.

✍

Over the next fifteen minutes, father and son barely exchanged a word. They both concentrated on opening the goose barnacles with their fingernails and wolfing them down before they got cold. Caldas closed his eyes every time he put one in his mouth, as if the briny flavour of the black crustaceans might evaporate through his eyes if he kept them open.

Once the sole was on the table, the inspector's father expatiated on how stupid, in his view, it was to live in the city, and how people slip into moral decline when they lack the time to enjoy a glass of wine in the shade. He'd found his son a bit depressed, and put it down to the city rush, the noise and the toxic fumes from the cars.

The inspector didn't want to worry him further by adding that, barring a miracle, he'd just ruined his career in the police force. He listened quietly as his father told him that some recent rains had coincided with the flowering of the vine, making trouble for the following harvest. The autumn harvest, he lamented, would be smaller than previous ones.

'God will have to do something about it,' he said with a serious expression. 'Less wine means less happiness in the world.'

'By the way, yesterday I saw Ramón Ríos at Riofarma,' interrupted Leo. 'He asked me if there's a chance you might send him a crate before it's sold out. It seems he ordered a couple last year, but in the end he never received them.'

'Does he do an honest day's work these days?'

'Sometimes he does and sometimes he doesn't. You know, he takes his time. So anyway, what about the wine?'

'Tell me where I should send the crate and I'll do it as soon as I get back to the vineyard.'

Leo Caldas nodded and grabbed his mobile.

'If you don't mind, I'll ask him for the address now. That way you can sort it out yourselves without me in the middle,' said Caldas as he dialled his friend's number.

'Hi, Moncho, it's me, Leo. Is this a bad time?'

'Not at all. I'm only working,' joked Ríos.

Caldas was glad to find someone in a good mood amidst the tempest which seemed about to blow up over him.

'I've got my father here. He's asking me where you'd like to have that wine sent. Riofarma?'

'No way. This place is full of thieves. I'd rather he sent it to my home. And could I have two crates?' he added, and dictated his details.

'Well, that was all, really...' said Caldas after writing down the address on the back of a card. 'And thanks again for your help. Isidro Freire was very kind to us, and gave us all the information we needed.'

'You know, this morning I wanted to ask him what he'd thought of the man from *Patrol on the Air* in person, but I couldn't find him. Apparently he hasn't come to the lab. I hope you haven't scared him away,' said Ramón Ríos in a humorous tone.

'I don't think so, Moncho. Perhaps he's followed your example and jumped on a boat with a mermaid.'

'Well, I don't know about Freire, but in ten minutes I am repeating yesterday's sexy naval shenanigans.'

Leo Caldas's father had fond memories of the disobedient child who, despite being from a different background, had spent so much time with his son.

'What was that crazy bugger saying?' he asked as Leo put the phone on the table.

'The usual nonsense,' replied Leo, and passed his father the card with the address where the wine should be sent. 'And a guy I saw yesterday at Riofarma has not turned up for work today, so Moncho was blaming me for his absence.'

'As eccentric as ever,' smiled his father.

Leo looked at his watch. It was past four.

'Are you going back to the vineyard? After lunch, I mean.'

'Yes, I finished my errands here this morning. You know, the less time I spend in the city the better.'

'Would you mind dropping me off a bit beyond the station? You'll have to make a detour, but that way we'll have more time to finish our lunch and I'll save myself the walk uphill on a full stomach.'

'Sure,' his father agreed. 'I've got nothing else to do. Where are you going?'

'I've arranged to meet someone for work at the cafeteria of the Mexico Hotel,' he said, steering clear of any specifics. 'I don't want my assistant to be there before me, as you never know what might happen when he's on his own.'

His father nodded. He'd heard how impetuous his son's new subordinate could be.

'Talking of being on your own – is Alba back at home yet?'

'No,' said Caldas, staring at the sole. 'She's not coming back.'

↝

They drove uphill away from the *ría*. They passed the train station on their left, and kept on climbing with the traffic towards the aptly-named *Calvario* – Stations of the Cross. They had to dodge a few barriers marking off potholes, which were already part of the urban scenery. The inspector's father was flabbergasted at how pedestrians negotiated the obstacles on the pavements while sweating under the fierce afternoon sun.

'One day you'll have to explain to me what stuff these people take to be able to go on living here, Leo.'

The inspector refrained from reminding him that he had spent several decades himself in the city he now loathed. Caldas just kept silent, hoping his father wouldn't ask him any questions concerning his job or insist on discussing his relationship with Alba.

He checked his watch and saw it was two minutes past five. He was late for his appointment with the DJ from the Idílico.

'In the countryside you can watch the days go by,' speechified his father. 'Here, apart from the fact that you're surrounded by all this rubbish, you rush through the days without seeing anything. Haven't you thought of that, Leo? I bet you've never thought of that.'

'When you put it that way...' replied Calda tersely.

'Do think about it.'

'I'll get out here,' said the inspector, seeing an opportunity now the car had stopped at a red light, 'so you don't have to turn round and can escape even sooner.'

'Already?' asked his father, surprised at his sudden farewell. 'When will you come down to visit me, Leo?'

For no particular reason, the inspector usually lied when he said goodbye to his father. But this time he thought he might be making an accurate prediction about how soon he'd have some time off.

'Next week I'll come to the vineyard.'

'Promise?' his father asked him, as if he were still a child.

'I'm afraid so,' he said, opening the door. 'I'm pretty sure I'll find the time.'

'Leo!' his father stopped him before he got out and, as he turned round, added: 'You know, it's not good to be alone.'

The inspector gave him a hug, and closed the door behind him.

The traffic lights turned green, and several drivers started beeping their horns so that the ones ahead would move.

Leo Caldas saw his father lose himself in the traffic, and wondered whether he might not be right.

Encouragement

It was the hour for the sports talk show on Radio Vigo, and the presenter greeted the audience while the theme tune played out.

Caldas, who'd sat by one of the windows overlooking the station, was the only customer at the cafeteria. The hotel's guests were either out visiting the city or keeping away from the heat in their air-conditioned rooms. Caldas stared at the trains going past the Soviet-looking concrete buildings that someone with dubious taste had erected many years before. At least, he thought, they hadn't built a Volkhaus to match.

He kept looking at his watch. He was hoping this talk with Orestes, the shaven-headed DJ from the Idílico, might offer a few leads to help him solve the murder of Luis Reigosa as speedily as possible.

He'd been waiting impatiently for over half an hour when, through the window, he saw his assistant galloping like a crazed rhino. Estévez looked exhausted. The effort of hauling his bulk up the hill at such a pace had obviously been too much. Estévez glanced about the tables and, when he located the inspector, walked over, with no time to catch his breath.

'Fucking hills!' he said. The police officer was sweating like a horse, and he gasped as he talked. 'Didn't you say it was only a little way uphill from the station, chief?'

The inspector pointed to the station through the window; the trains were in plain view.

'I know where it is, damn it, that's where I came from. But you didn't say I had to climb three hundred steps afterwards.' He was so short of breath he had to pause again. 'We're always in a rush, everything's uphill, and, to make matters worse, today the weather is treacherously hot and sticky.'

Estévez pulled the collar of his corduroy shirt, unsuccessfully trying to put a bit of air between it and his body. He checked the watch on his left wrist. They'd arranged to meet at five and it was quarter to six.

'*And* I'm late. Shit!'

'No, you're on time,' corrected the inspector.

'Hasn't the DJ turned up yet?'

'What do you think?' asked Caldas.

'For God's sake, chief, enough with the cryptic messages, I've run all the way from down there,' he said, pointing to the trains. 'Has he not come at all or has he left already?'

'I got here a little after five, and there was no one here then. I guess he hasn't come.' The inspector looked around the empty cafeteria. 'I guess he won't come,' he added to himself.

'Well you could have told me, chief. I would've driven up and parked the car nearby, even if it took longer to find a space.'

Estévez turned to the bar and raised a hand.

'Waiter! A Coke with lots of ice, please!' he roared, taking the menu from the table and waving it in the air. 'Have you had any thoughts about what we're doing next?'

Caldas eyed him in silence, with a musing look.

'Me and you,' insisted a bad-tempered Estévez. 'Have you thought how we're going to get out of this one? Because I guess it won't be long before Superintendent Soto learns that a pair of stupid officers have been bullying none other than Doctor Zuriaga,' he said.

Caldas listened as if he didn't really care.

'No.'

'You'd better think up something, chief, because they're going to crucify us. I mean, I'm used to it, but God knows where they'll send me this time... I'll end up as a forest ranger on the Chafarina Islands, alone with the bloody seals.'

Estévez wiped the sweat off his forehead with his hand.

'Besides, I'm annoyed that his niece will not like the way things are going,' he added.

'Whose niece?' asked Caldas, as if he didn't understand.

'Who do you think? You know damn well, chief. Zuriaga's.'

Estévez was fanning his huge belly with the menu.

'Is that Coke coming or not?' he shouted towards the bar. Leo Caldas smiled.

'What's so funny?' asked Estévez.

Caldas answered with a grin still on his face:

'Nothing.'

'How do you mean, nothing? What struck you as so irresistibly funny, inspector?'

'It's nothing, Rafa.' Caldas shook his head. 'Our career's on the line and you worry about Diana. Diana Zuriaga, no less. As if you stood a chance anyway.'

Rafael brought down the menu on the table with a bang that, in the empty cafeteria, sounded like a shot.

'Look, let me remind you that, firstly, it was *your* suicidal tendencies that landed us in all this trouble – and then they call me the crazy one. Secondly, I'll worry about whomever I damn well please.' Caldas was about to say something, but the officer, who had put out two fingers, uncurled a third without letting him. 'Thirdly, it's a moot point whether I stand a chance with that girl. I know perfectly well that I'm a few years older, and a good deal heavier than her, and that I'm probably not classy enough to be his driver.' He took a breath. 'But I've as much right as anyone else to build my hopes up with whomever I like without anyone mocking me, whether he is a superior or not. Do you get me, inspector?'

'I wasn't mocking you, Rafa.' His smile had disappeared during his assistant's tirade.

'But you were, inspector, you were,' spat Estévez, whose agitation made him sweat even more. 'Do you think I don't know that smug little grin of yours?'

Caldas remained silent, and Estévez, turning to the waiter, bellowed:

'And you, will you bring me that bloody Coke today, or do I have to go and get it myself?'

The waiter sprang up from behind the bar and brought the drink in one hand and a glass in the other. He left them on the table, as near as possible to the impatient policeman.

'Don't be so touchy, Rafa. I didn't mean to...' said the inspector by way of excuse once his assistant seemed a bit calmer.

'Let's drop it, inspector. It's too hot to get upset.'

Estévez grabbed the Coke to pour it into the glass, and turned to face the waiter.

'Where's the ice?'

'Is it not cold enough?' the waiter asked.

'I don't know.' Rafael Estévez didn't feel the need to explain. 'I want it with ice.'

The waiter saw things differently.

'I've just taken it out of the fridge. Look,' he said, taking the bottle and moving it nearer to the officer, who smacked at the glass and gave him a furious look.

'I don't give a fuck how cold it is or if a penguin brought it all the way from the South Pole. Bring me some bloody ice,' he ordered, making a huge effort to remain seated.

The waiter touched the bottle with the palm of his hand as if to prove it was positively glacial.

'I said with ice!' shouted Estévez, out of control.

The inspector didn't dare ask him to keep his voice down. The unflagging waiter, however, seemed determined to use his powers of persuasion, and moved the bottle a bit closer to the officer.

'If you want ice, I'll bring you ice, but check how chilled it is.'

Estévez stood up, grabbed the waiter by the neck, and proceeded to shake him this way and that.

'I want it with ice, lots of ice! Do you get me?' he shouted heatedly. 'You pigheaded buffoon, you Galician son of a bitch!'

Leo Caldas jumped up and gripped his angry assistant's arm.

'What's wrong with you, Rafa, are you insane? And you,' he ordered, 'just bring that ice, will you? You're even crazier than he is.'

The waiter, paralysed with fear, nodded slowly. As soon as Estévez let go of him, he ran off to the bar. He came back bringing a small metal bucket filled to the brim with ice cubes.

⌢

Leo Caldas and Rafael Estévez sat in silence for a few minutes. The inspector smoked a couple of cigarettes looking out of the window, while the officer rested his sweat-drenched forehead on his hands.

Once the mood had improved, Caldas tried to put his thoughts in order and go over ideas that might cast some light on the case. None of them made much sense. But then, remembering his lunch with his father, and the telephone conversation he'd had with Moncho Ríos, it struck him as curious that Isidro Freire had skipped work that day. It was easy to assume he was ill, but there were other possibilities that might explain his absence: he might be scared, as Moncho Ríos had jokingly suggested, or someone might have made him disappear in order to silence him.

'Aren't you going?' Estévez suddenly asked, lifting his head and looking at the inspector.

'Where?'

'The radio, chief,' said Estévez, pointing to the loudspeaker hanging from the ceiling. 'They've just announced your show. It's starting in half an hour.'

'Shit!' muttered Leo looking at his watch. He'd forgotten his programme was on that afternoon. He'd been hearing the radio in the background all this time, as if it were the sound-track of a film, without paying attention to anything but his own musings.

'Rafa, are you OK?' asked Caldas with concern. He was still disconcerted by his assistant's fiery reaction.

Officer Estévez confirmed he was.

'I'll push off then. Wait here a bit longer,' asked the inspector. 'If Orestes doesn't show up, go and find him. We can't afford to lose him.'

'And where shall I go and find him, as you put it?'

'I don't know really. The Idílico if it's open, his house... Perhaps they know something about him at the station – they know a lot of people who work in bars and suchlike. If you'd rather not drive, take a taxi wherever you need to go and we can claim it as expenses.'

Estévez rested his forehead on his open palms once again.

'Rafa, I'm sorry about earlier.' Caldas regretted saying this as soon as he started the sentence. 'But we have to go on. This is quite possibly our last chance to dig ourselves out of this one.'

Estévez lifted his head and grabbed the bottle of Coke, which had remained untouched on the table.

'You sure you're OK?' repeated the inspector as he got ready to leave.

Rafael reassured him and Caldas patted him on the back.

He was opening the door when he heard the waiter.

'Are you leaving your friend on his own?' he asked anxiously.

Refuge

Leo Caldas went into the building across from Plaza de la Alameda, greeted the caretaker, quickly climbed the staircase and, once on the first floor, pushed open a door. He walked down the long corridor to the sound booth, hearing the music Radio Vigo was playing in the background.

'Hello, inspector,' greeted the technician sitting in front of the sound console as he came in.

'Good evening.'

Caldas, pausing under the cold jet coming from the air-conditioning, saw it was already five past seven, and read on the thermometer that the temperature outside was thirty-two degrees. He recalled Estévez's soaked corduroy shirt and reckoned he would have been very glad to stand there just then. Rebeca and Santiago Losada were chatting in the studio on the other side of the glass. The presenter, with his headphones round his neck, seemed worried at the producer's words.

Caldas knocked on the glass and both heads turned at once. Rebeca smiled at him, but Losada pointed angrily to the digital clock on the wall, and signalled frantically for him to come into the studio without delay. Caldas met Rebeca at the soundproofed door.

'Where were you, Leo? I've been calling you on your mobile for over an hour.'

'Work,' replied Caldas dryly.

'And what about the messages on your voicemail? Leo, you're a complete disaster.'

'The battery must have run out,' lied the inspector, who had turned off the phone at the restaurant after talking to Ramón Ríos.

'You'd better go in. The media man in there almost suffered a heart attack when you didn't turn up. He can do most of the show, you know, but he needs you for this one thing...'

Leo Caldas slipped into the studio and took his usual seat, the one nearer the window.

'You're late,' was Losada's welcoming greeting.

'I am.'

Rebeca spoke over the interphone.

'Santiago, shall we start *Patrol* or do you want me to play another song?'

'Enough songs. Let's take those calls,' rushed Losada.

'By the way, Leo,' continued Rebeca, 'Superintendent Soto seems to want to speak to you pretty urgently. He's called here a dozen times. It seems he hasn't been able to contact you on your mobile either.'

Exactly why I switched it off, Leo said to himself.

'Thanks, Rebeca.'

Caldas could predict that future conversation with Soto as if he had the gift of foresight, and he wasn't at all interested in facing his superior's accusing shouts – not without first gathering some reasons that might explain why he had harassed Zuriaga. What was worse, he wasn't sure he'd be able to gather them in time. Zuriaga was too powerful and would surely move quickly. Besides, the small hope that Orestes represented had dissolved like sugar in a glass of warm milk. He needed to speak to the DJ, and though Rafael would do anything in his power to find him, the officer wasn't exactly a discreet man, and was not familiar with the ins and outs of the city. Not by a long way. Orestes would see him coming a mile off, and would disappear again, leaving them exposed to any legal action that the doctor might want to bring against them.

Santiago Losada raised his hand and the theme tune of the programme rolled around the studio. Through the window Caldas saw the mothers talking in the square. They had chosen the shade under the trees for their daily gathering. The children ignored the heat and chased the pigeons, frightening them away in their daily hunting session. The birds waited until the last possible moment before they took flight.

Caldas thought of Alba. She too had flown, she had escaped when he thought she was closest to him.

Santiago lowered his hand, and with that movement the melody faded out and a red light came on in the studio, indicating that they were now on the air.

'Ladies and gentlemen, now with us... *Patrol on the Air*. The forum where the voice of the citizens meets the voice of public order with one goal – to improve the way we all live together in our beloved city.' Santiago Losada paused theatrically in mid presentation.

Leo Caldas turned to the table and picked up the uncomfortable headphones, waiting for the first call before putting them on.

The presenter carried on as if he were the MC at a boxing match and he was introducing one of the pugilists.

'And now, here with us, the criminals' nemesis, the unflagging defender of the good citizen, the fearsome guardian of our homes, the patrolman – Inspector Leo Caldas. Good evening, inspector.'

Not for long, thought Caldas, and replied: 'Good evening.'

'Inspector Caldas is here at Radio Vigo to assist you with any problems you may have, dear listeners, on this *Patrol on the Air* we've created for your benefit.'

Rebeca put up a sign and Losada took the call.

'Inés is the first one today to seek the protection of the law. Good evening,' he greeted her, and the long-suffering inspector put on the headphones.

After a polite greeting, the woman specified the reason she was calling. It was a traffic matter that she described in a vague manner. In any case, it was the responsibility of the Municipal Police.

Caldas wrote down: one-nil.

↩

After half an hour, his black-covered notebook recorded the depressing score of: Municipal Police seven – Leo nil.

Rebeca, in the control room, showed the sign with another name on it: Carlos.

'I'm calling to express our strongest condemnation of the aggression that a member of our community endured yesterday, 13 May, during his leisure time at a bar in our city.' The man spoke without pausing to breathe. He was obviously reading from a text.

'Do you want to lodge a complaint with Inspector Caldas?' asked Losada.

'That won't be necessary.' Carlos's voice sounded a bit more camp when he wasn't reading. 'He was at that bar drinking a beer and was able to take it all in with his own eyes.'

Leo moved his mouth away from the microphone, trying to find mental shelter in the sunny view of the Alameda square.

'Shit! That's all we needed now!' he muttered.

'In fact,' the listener went on, 'it was Inspector Caldas himself who came to the rescue of the assaulted man, overpowered the homophobe and threw him out of the bar.'

'Did he now?'

Losada's sarcasm invited the caller to carry on. The man provided a detailed account of what had happened the night before, launched into vigorous criticism of public institutions that allowed animals such as the aggressor to be a part of their security forces, and rounded off by demanding that the responsible parties be held accountable for this. The impassioned Carlos didn't fail to thank Inspector Caldas properly for what he considered 'heroic behaviour in favour of our complete integration'.

Throughout the speech, Leo Caldas repeatedly mimed a pair of scissors with his index and middle fingers up in the air, motioning Losada to cut the call. However, in a surprising democratic gesture, Santiago Losada allowed his exalted listener to finish his plea.

As soon as the ads came on, the inspector took the chance to demand an explanation.

'Why did you let him go on? We're not supposed to make people afraid of the police here. Quite the opposite.'

'Freedom of expression comes first,' Losada justified himself.

'Freedom? I didn't know that was a word in your vocabulary.'

'You're just angry because he's revealed on air that you were in such a peculiar bar,' said Losada, in a deliberately impertinent tone, 'but what's the problem? Our society has grown, and now accepts any orientation.'

'Do me a favour, Santiago – go to hell.'

Caldas gave the presenter a scornful look, put a cigarette in his mouth and touched the flame of the lighter to it.

'Nuria, good evening. You are through to *Patrol on the Air*, the forum presided over by the incorruptible Inspector Leo Caldas,' greeted Losada, glancing at Caldas with an insolent look.

The ninth caller of the evening shared with them the story of how frightened she felt at night, as over the past two weeks a couple of lowlifes had taken to sleeping in the hall of her building.

Breaking and entering was indeed the inspector's responsibility, and he picked up his pen to record one point. Seven–one.

In spite of the headphones, he heard a thud over the high-pitched voice of the caller. He raised his eyes and saw Rafael Estévez in the next room, knocking on the glass very near him. Rebeca and the sound technician did not interfere with him, and looked on as frightened as they were surprised. The officer, gesturing wildly, was asking Caldas to come and speak to him at once. And just at the moment when the caller was enquiring what the solution was, Caldas left the studio without Losada's noticing.

'Well, inspector?' asked the presenter, foolishly looking at the empty seat to his right.

'They've wiped him out, chief. He won't talk now,' blurted Estévez in the sound booth, his face all flushed.

'What?'

'I found the DJ at home. He's dead,' explained the officer. 'I've been trying to contact you for an hour. Is your mobile off?'

'Yes. Who else knows of this?' asked Caldas.

'Just you and me.'

'Let's go then,' he said, and they made for the street.

On the loudspeaker in the corridor they heard Losada, on the brink of a nervous breakdown, pretending the caller had been cut off and presenting a ridiculous song.

Impression

The block of flats on Avenida de las Camelias was one of those functional buildings that multinational companies with branches in the city rented for employees who were transferred to Vigo. It was cheaper for those companies to keep a number of flats all year round than to finance their executives' numerous nights in hotels one by one.

Caldas and Estévez got out of the taxi, went into the hall and climbed up the stairs to the fifth floor. Estévez stopped in front of a door with a small brass plaque that read Orestes Grial.

'And this?' asked the inspector. As he pushed the door, he noticed the lock was smashed.

'I rang the bell,' said Estévez by way of an excuse, 'and as nobody answered I kicked it a bit and...'

'I see.'

The inspector took a quick look at the empty flat. A single large room, with dark floorboards and white walls, served as living room, dining area and bedroom. The modern open-plan kitchen was next to one of the two windows overlooking the street. On the shelves on the wall were a dozen books, two photo albums, a digital camera and a few hundred CDs. Everything was neat and tidy, except for the unmade, pillow-less bed.

'Where is he?'

'In there,' replied Estévez, pointing to a closed door.

Caldas went into the bathroom and found Orestes spread-eagled on the floor by the toilet bowl. He'd bled from the back of his shaven head and the blood had spread into a red puddle, which contrasted sharply with the white marble – an unsettling sight.

The DJ was wearing only striped pyjama-bottoms, and his bare chest revealed how thin he was. The pillow was on the floor, stained with blood.

'Did you move anything?'

'Of course not. After I found the stiff and called you eighty times on your mobile, I made sure there was no one else here, pulled the door shut and went to get you at the radio station.'

Leo Caldas inspected the hole the bullet had made in the back of the boy's neck. He didn't want to touch the wound, and with all the blood he wasn't able to calculate the calibre of the gun. He tried to locate the shell of the bullet on the floor, also unsuccessfully. As he was looking for it, he lifted the pillow slightly by one of its cleanest corners, and saw a hole going through it surrounded by a blackish stain. The murderer had used the pillow to muffle the shot. He pointed it out to Estévez.

'I noticed that already, chief,' said the officer. 'A home-made silencer, but an efficient one nonetheless.'

Caldas left the pillow on the floor. No sign of the shell.

'They caught him pissing,' said Estévez.

Caldas nodded.

'Perhaps the doorbell woke him up,' he speculated. 'He must have got up to go and open the door, and then he needed to urinate.'

⤺

They decided to look for clues on their own before calling anyone in from the police station. Caldas, using a handkerchief to make sure he didn't leave any fingerprints, turned the digital camera on and saw its memory was empty. Then he concentrated on the albums on the shelf. Meanwhile Estévez, who had put on a pair of gloves he'd found in the kitchen sink, carried out a search round the flat. He went through the night-table, the table in the living room, the cushions on the sofa, the kitchen… Then he opened the wardrobe, rifled through its drawers one by one, and checked the pockets of all the trousers and jackets on the hangers.

Caldas devoted his time to looking through the first of the photo albums. He scrutinised every picture with a watch-maker's meticulousness, but he didn't find any known faces there. He put it back on the shelf, next to the CDs, and reached for the second one.

Estévez drew near to take a look at the CDs. Almost all of them were copies, with the artists' names written in indelible ink.

'Do you realise? Only idiots buy CDs these days. At this rate, a plumber will soon make more money than a rock star,' declared Estévez sententiously.

'Indeed,' muttered Caldas, engrossed in the photographs.

Estévez went over the CDs hastily, and looked around as if something were missing.

'Where the hell did he play them?' he asked, thinking out loud.

'What?' asked Caldas without taking his eyes off a photo-graph taken at the Idílico.

'Nothing, it's there,' said Estévez, calmly looking at the kitchen. 'I was wondering where he played the CDs, but it must be on that laptop.'

'What did you say?' asked Caldas, raising his eyes.

'That he must have listened to his CDs on that computer there in the kitchen,' repeated Estévez.

Leo Caldas had already noticed the flat object on the kitchen surface near the cooker, but he thought it must be a sandwich maker or some such appliance. Nor had the gizmo which sat right next to it on a stack of garish paper attracted his attention.

He went over to the kitchen surface, opened the laptop, and turned it on. The futuristic object to the right turned out to be a small laser printer sitting on a ream of paper.

As the computer started up and logged on its profiles, the inspector finished checking the second album; he didn't find anything of interest there either, and returned to the shelf.

He went back to the keyboard and opened the recent-items menu. He saw that the last programmes used were the web browser and the image processor. He clicked on the latter, and accessed another complex menu. The inspector was no expert in new technologies, but was familiar enough with computers to realise that Orestes kept thousands of digital photographs stored on the hard drive of his.

There was a search option on that screen allowing you to set parameters in order to find certain files more quickly. Leo Caldas wrote the name he was looking for: Luis Reigosa.

A moment later twelve icons showed up. He clicked on the first, and a photo opened at once, filling the screen.

'Bingo!' said the inspector.

Rafael Estévez approached.

'What's up, chief?'

Leo Caldas didn't reply. He kept opening the images and pressing the print key.

'They knew each other,' muttered Estévez, with his eyes riveted on the first picture that came out of the printer. 'Son of a bitch!'

Trace

The wooden gate slid to one side, and the car advanced among the trees before stopping in front of the steps. The maid was waiting for the officers in the same martial posture she'd adopted in the morning, and led them round the house to the porch just like before.

Yet things were different. The sun wasn't high in the sky but setting over a shimmering sea that seemed covered in gold leaf, and to Estévez's relief the temperature had dropped a few degrees since noon. The officer was no longer sweating.

On the path leading to the quay, they saw the slender Mercedes Zuriaga silhouetted against a background of bright light. She had put a long white chemise over her cream dress. She went past them and stopped as she recognised them.

'Good evening, officers. Another visit?' she asked politely.

'Yes, we need the doctor's advice once again,' lied Caldas.

'Does he know you're here?'

Leo nodded.

'I was about to ask for some tea,' she said, pointing to the sliding door leading into the living room. 'Would you like a cup?'

They said no, thank you.

Merecedes Zuriaga disappeared into the living room for a minute, and after giving some terse instructions, came back and sat down with them under the porch. A little later, the maid in the cap appeared carrying a small silver tray and left it on the table.

'If it's all right, I'll keep you company until my husband comes down.'

'Of course,' agreed Caldas. 'Is the doctor feeling better?'

'It would seem so. A little after you left he went out on some errands and to do a bit of shopping,' she explained. 'It's a good sign if he's in the mood to spend money,' she joked.

'Naturally,' admitted Caldas.

'Are you sure you won't have any tea?' she insisted, lifting the teapot.

Caldas and Estévez thanked her, but again declined. The three of them sat there, appreciating the view and hearing the sea hit the rocks as Mercedes Zuriaga stirred her tea with a spoon.

↜

When the doctor came out and approached the porch, Caldas experienced that gut feeling he'd missed in the morning. Now the sun was lower, the bougainvillea didn't cast a shadow, and Dimas Zuriaga's hair looked as immaculately white as Caldas had seen it at the cemetery.

'Inspector Caldas, I thought I made things perfectly clear this morning,' said Zuriaga without hiding his exasperation.

Leo didn't want to elaborate in front of his wife.

'Rafa, would you mind sitting with Mrs Zuriaga while I take a stroll with the doctor?' asked Caldas.

↜

They walked away in silence. The inspector pointed to a stone table far from the porch, near the pond-turned-swimming-pool.

'Would you mind if we sit down over there, doctor?'

Dimas Zuriaga reluctantly agreed and, once they'd done so, asked Caldas what exactly was expected from him.

'An honest answer,' replied Caldas, placing on the table the photograph of Luis Reigosa and his saxophone, the same he'd showed Zuriaga that morning. 'Do you know this man?'

Zuriaga didn't even look at the picture.

'They promised me this morning's outrage wouldn't be repeated,' said the doctor dryly. 'You've justified your impertinence as best you could, and I vouchsafed to forget the incident. But this is too much.'

'Do you know him?' pressed Caldas.

'Do you think I'm one of those petty criminals you can bully just like that?' exclaimed Zuriaga, standing up.

Leo made an effort to remain calm.

'I don't think anything, doctor, but let me assure you I'm treating you with far more respect than I think you deserve in the circumstances. For the last time, then, do you know this man?'

'I've said I don't!' roared Zuriaga in his thunderous voice. 'Now get out of my house, please.'

Leo Caldas took another photograph from the inside pocket of his jacket. In it, Dimas Zuriaga and Luis Reigosa were having an animated conversation with two beer glasses in front of them. Caldas placed it on the table, very near the doctor.

'What do you say now, do you know him?'

He took out another picture and threw it on the table.

'Do you know who I mean or would you rather think it over, doctor?'

Leo threw another photograph in the air. This one left no doubts as to the kind of relationship between the doctor and the saxophonist.

'Are you not saying anything, doctor?'

Dima Zuriaga, suddenly pale, sat back down. He held the photographs in his hand for a moment and then dropped them on the table.

'You don't need to show me all of them, inspector. I know these pictures.' There was no trace of his former defiance.

'So you do know the man who's in them with you?' asked Caldas once again.

'Of course I do, inspector,' he said at last. 'It's Luis. Luis Reigosa.'

'I don't like to be lied to, doctor,' said Caldas, fixing his eyes on Zuriaga.

'Why didn't you tell me from the start that you knew all

131

about it, inspector?' His roaring voice had turned into a whimper.

'About what?' Leo Caldas didn't know what he meant exactly, but he encouraged him to carry on.

'The blackmail. Isn't that the reason you're here? Someone's been emailing me pictures like this one for a while now. I thought no one else knew about them.'

It wasn't such a strange reply as it might first seem. People involved in crimes would often cast themselves as victims in a last attempt to confuse their pursuers. Leo decided to follow the thread the doctor was offering and see where it was leading. Dimas Zuriaga was too important a personage for the inspector's career to suffer another setback.

'Did you report it, doctor?'

Dimas Zuriaga shook his head, and as he did the sun glinted on his white hair as on a mirror.

'They threatened to forward them to my wife if I went to the police,' the doctor glanced furtively at the table in the porch, where his wife and Rafael Estévez were still sitting. 'She knows nothing about this,' he added.

'Would you rather we walked where they can't see us, doctor?'

Zuriaga nodded and Caldas indicated the path leading to the quay.

'No, let's go the other way, inspector. I only like the sea from afar. I've been afraid of the water since I was small – I don't even know how to swim.'

'And the boat?' asked Caldas.

'That's Mercedes's. I don't go near it.'

Zuriaga pointed to a path leading to the forest they'd seen from the entrance.

'This way.'

The path went round a pond and led into a copse of old chestnut trees. As he waited for the doctor to start talking, Caldas walked silently, surrounded by vegetable smells which were stronger under the trees.

'I got the first pictures one Monday morning, about a month ago,' he finally said. 'They asked me for three thousand euros to destroy them. I had to leave the money at a certain spot on Monte del Castro, near the Foundation.'

'And did you pay?'

'I did, but the following Monday I got another email, and the following week another... In total I left three envelopes in that place.'

'Did you ever consider reporting it to the police?'

'I though of it, but then I convinced myself that it would be more discreet to engage a private detective. I was considering different alternatives, but as you know when one has too many options it becomes difficult to choose from them, inspector. The money they were asking for was not excessive – I mean, not for someone in my position. And I couldn't make a mistake with a matter such as this one. So I didn't mind holding out for a while and paying up until I found the right person to take care of the investigation. I was going to engage someone as soon as I received the next message, but last Monday I didn't get any pictures.'

'And you decided to hide it all in case that was it.'

'Exactly, inspector. There didn't seem to be any point in stirring things up just for the sake of it. I try not to attract any notice, but I can't help being a public figure. Few people in this city know my face, but they all know my name and that of the organisation I represent. I couldn't let a scandal of this sort taint the Foundation.'

'Or your family.'

'Indeed. It's all connected – work, family, society... A scandal could shake everything I and my father before me have worked for.'

Leo Caldas was thinking that the doctor's words would need solid evidence to back them up.

'Did you keep the messages, doctor?'

'No. I did for a few days, but then I deleted them.'

You're not very lucky, thought Caldas.

'I see. Who could have taken those pictures?'

'I don't know, inspector, I have no idea.'

'And sent them?'

'The same,' replied Zuriaga. 'I don't know a great deal about computers, but I did look into it. The email addresses from which they were sent were fakes and had absurd names. All I was able to find out was that they were sent from cyber cafes, which hundreds of people use every day.'

'Do you know that Reigosa is dead, doctor?'

'Of course. I was at his funeral yesterday – just like you, inspector. As I told you this morning, I hardly ever forget a face.'

The path passed under magnolia, yew and pine trees. Where it forked Zuriaga took the right.

'Did you ever suspect it might have been Reigosa who was blackmailing you?'

'Are you mad? Why would Luis do something like that?'

'Don't you think it's a bit odd that you stopped receiving emails just when he died?'

'It isn't.' There was no sign of hesitation in Dimas Zuriaga's voice. 'Luis only had to ask for whatever he needed. A man like him wouldn't do such a stupid thing as blackmailing me for money. You've seen the pictures. You know about me, about us, inspector.'

Leo nodded, but Zuriaga laboured the point.

'We were more than friends. I would have given him anything he might have needed without even asking him what it was for. He had no reason to do something like that.'

'Did you do it?'

'Do what?'

'Give him money.'

'God, no, of course I didn't.' The doctor drew his hand over his white hair. 'But I would've done if he'd asked.'

'Was he that important to you?'

'You don't understand, inspector.'

'That's why we're having this conversation, doctor, so you

can explain to me what I don't understand. Was he *that* important?' he insisted.

'Of course, he was more important than even he suspected.'

'But not enough to leave your wife.'

'I've already explained to you what I represent, inspector. A great enterprise like the Zuriaga Foundation requires that one should make certain sacrifices. I chose to lead this horrid double life. I chose to deceive Mercedes all this time.'

'And was it worth it?'

'Well, actually, I think it was, inspector. At least, that was the idea, even if at times I was tempted to openly speak to her about my... shall we say, inclination.'

'Why didn't you?' asked Caldas.

'Tell Mercedes? For several reasons, but in the first place, because Luis wouldn't let me. He encouraged me to carry on with my main projects – the Foundation and my marriage.'

They walked and talked like Peripatetics, along the path bordering on a coppice of box trees. Caldas listened to Zuriaga's explanations with the feeling that he was before a crumbling giant.

'How long have you led this double life, doctor?'

'In a way I've always known, but I didn't take the plunge until Luis turned up. I've never wanted to go to a certain type of bar. I'm too old to brandish a flag or mix in some absurd, superficial ambiance.'

This man with snow-white hair had little in common with the one who'd called to denounce Estévez's misconduct at the Idílico.

'Could I ask you how you met Reigosa?'

'At a jazz festival sponsored by the Foundation. We talked after the concert, then there was a dinner party and then...'

'When was that?'

'About three years ago.'

'And are you sure your wife doesn't suspect anything? Three years is a long time.'

'Mercedes? No, I don't think so. I've never been a model husband. Always too busy for that.'

'You do know Reigosa was killed, don't you, doctor?'

'Since his death I've been terribly depressed, cut off from the world. I've only left the house to go to the cemetery,' he said.

Caldas thought Zuriaga hadn't proved so depressed when it came to complaining to Caldas's superiors.

'Do you know what formaldehyde is?'

'Inspector, you're talking to a doctor who's head of a hospital. Of course I know what formaldehyde is.'

'They used it to kill Reigosa.'

'Did they put him to sleep?'

'Not exactly.'

He didn't want to explain any further. He'd have time during the interrogation at the station. He had enough on Zuriaga.

'Shall we go back?'

⁓

They did so in silence. The afternoon sun penetrated into the undergrowth, and the shadows of the trees made strange patterns on the ground. As the sun went down, the smell of the plants grew stronger.

When they were near the house, the inspector decided to round off with one last question.

'Does the name Orestes Grial ring a bell?'

'No.'

'Take your time, doctor. You've already lied once.'

The comment visibly annoyed Dimas Zuriaga.

'I don't know who Orestes is, inspector. I'm being honest with you now – there's no need for sarcasm.'

'Have you been here all day?' asked Caldas, changing his approach.

'I have indeed. I've already told you I haven't left my property in days. Why do you ask me about this Orestes chap now, inspector? What does he have to do with me?'

'Remember this morning I said I had a witness who knew about your relationship with Reigosa, doctor?'

'Yes.'

'Those photographs I've shown you, the same ones you said you've received before, were stored on Orestes Grial's computer. We should've talked to him today, but he wasn't able to come to our appointment. He was murdered. We found him in the bathroom of his flat. Someone shot him in the back of the neck when he was urinating. And the reason we were meeting, curiously enough, was to finish a conversation we'd started the day before on the subject of Reigosa.'

'Luis?'

'Do you know what the Idílico is, doctor?'

'Yes, a gay bar, but as I've said I don't go to that kind of place.'

'Not you, but it seems your friend Reigosa dropped by every now and then. The boy who was killed worked there as a DJ.'

Zuriaga was listening carefully.

'Where are you going with all this, inspector?'

'I don't believe in coincidences, doctor. I would like you to come with me to the police station to make a statement.'

'Are you arresting me?' stuttered Zuriaga.

'I won't handcuff you, if that's what you're afraid of, but you should be thinking about contacting your lawyer. Two deaths might prove too much, even for a man like yourself.'

'Two deaths?' Zuriaga looked at him imploringly. 'After what I've told you, you can't seriously think I've killed Luis or that lad.'

'I don't think anything, doctor. I'm only doing my job. And I'll be happy for you to prove your innocence. Of course, I could leave now without you, but with the evidence we've got I'd be forced to come back before long with an arrest warrant signed by a judge.'

The doctor remained silent for a moment, as if gauging

the situation. 'Let me get my coat,' he muttered with a resigned expression.

Caldas looked on as Dimas Zuriaga dragged his feet towards his majestic stone mansion.

'Doctor!' he called out.

Zuriaga stopped and turned round.

'If you want to speak to your wife... I'm not ruling out the possibility that nothing comes of this, but there's a chance it'll all get out. I think she'd be grateful if she heard it from you first.'

'I'm not sure she'll believe me,' the doctor confessed. 'But it'll be a relief to finally talk to Mercedes.'

Relationship

Once in the police station they accompanied Dimas Zuriaga to a meeting room. They left him sitting on a sofa and offered him a cup of coffee from the coffee machine. The doctor may be a suspect, but his eminence required the greatest courtesy.

Caldas and Estévez were summoned to Superintendent Soto's office.

'Will you tell me what the fuck Zuriaga's doing here?' greeted Soto with his usual kindness.

Estévez sighed nervously, and Caldas started to speak.

'It has to do with the death of Luis Reigosa, the musician who turned up murdered at the Toralla tower.'

'I know who Reigosa is,' cut in Soto. 'I'm asking what the hell Doctor Zuriaga's doing in my station. Do you know they expressly asked me to keep you away from him? Is this what you understand by staying away from someone?'

Estévez hung his head, but Caldas was undaunted.

'If it's any consolation, we haven't brought the doctor by force, sir. He decided to come with us of his own free will.'

'Of course he did. And I bet he also asked for a very dark cell,' spat Superintendent Soto, visibly agitated.

'Sir, may I explain why the doctor's here?' Leo waited for his superior's answer, but it didn't materialise. 'You may want to make something up when one of his minions, any moment now, calls up demanding an explanation.'

The superintendent sat down and pointed to the chairs on the other side of the desk.

'Go on,' he ordered, 'and keep it short.'

The policemen sat down. Caldas put a closed envelope on the desk and launched into his account.

'In a nutshell, Doctor Zuriaga had a relationship with Luis Reigosa for a couple of years...'

'A relationship?' interrupted Soto. 'What do you mean?'

'A relationship, sir, an... er... amorous relationship, if you want to call it that.'

'Give me a break, Leo,' exclaimed the superintendent, standing up and raising his arm in a theatrical display of disapproval. 'Let me remind you we're talking about Dimas Zuriaga.'

'May I explain it or not?' said Caldas tersely.

The superintendent, seeing the inspector's serious face, sat down again. Caldas interpreted this as a yes and started over.

'Zuriaga and Reigosa had been in a relationship for the last three years. A secret relationship, hidden from the eyes of society and even from the doctor's family. No one in his circle of friends and family knew of Reigosa's existence. Now, about a month ago the doctor started receiving anonymous emails. Those emails, which were sent from fake addresses, had explicit photographs attached of him and Reigosa. Whoever sent them asked him for money in exchange for not going public with the images. The doctor, who is of course a very discreet man, and was distressed at the possibility that his secret might come out, decided to pay up.'

Caldas, who played around with the envelope as he told his story, paused for a moment.

'So far, I've done nothing but relay what Zuriaga himself has told me,' he pointed out. 'The doctor can confirm it to the last word.'

'But where are you going with this, Leo?' asked Soto. 'You won't tell me you've brought the doctor in so he can report he's being blackmailed?'

'No, sir. He's here because we think he's involved in the death of the musician at the very least.'

'Have you not just told me he was his lover?' The superintendent was visibly reluctant to deal with a problem as big as the one posed by the Zuriaga Foundation. 'For the love of God, Leo...'

'I'm trying to be as clear as I can,' replied Caldas. 'Now let me tell you my theory.'

'Have you brought Zuriaga in on just a theory?'

Rafael Estévez fidgeted in his chair.

'For now it's only that,' confirmed Caldas.

'Shit, Leo, you'll be the ruin of me, of us all.'

Superintendent Soto buried his face in his hands for a moment. After vigorously rubbing his eyes he looked at Caldas.

'Go on,' he ordered dryly.

It was all that Caldas needed.

'Once he got over the shock of the first email, Zuriaga concentrated on finding the sender. He needed time, and so, week after week, for as long as the blackmail lasted, he paid as instructed. But a powerful man like Zuriaga, with enough resources to make people talk, ended up discovering who was behind the operation, and did so without arousing the blackmailer's suspicions. It took some time, four weeks or so, but he eventually found what he was after.'

Estévez and Soto listened attentively.

'Discovering the author of the blackmail was a far more painful blow to the doctor than actually being blackmailed,' carried on Leo, 'because behind the messages were the DJ of a gay bar – an amateur photographer – and none other than Reigosa, his lover.'

Soto opened his arms, demanding more explanations.

'The doctor's deepest secret had been betrayed by the person he trusted most,' went on Caldas, fighting interruptions. 'First he was devastated, but his confusion and depression soon turned into hatred and a desire for revenge. Luis Reigosa had played with Zuriaga's feelings and had taken advantage of them. The doctor wanted to get even, to cause as much pain as he had suddenly, and unexpectedly, suffered.'

'Can you prove any of this fairy tale?' asked Soto.

The inspector opened the envelope he had in his hands, and took out the pictures he had printed at Grial's flat.

'This morning when we first paid him a visit, the doctor assured us he didn't know Reigosa,' Caldas pointed out, as he laid out the compromising photographs on the table. 'Now he's saying he lied to cover up the blackmail and keep the pictures secret.'

Caldas allowed a puzzled Soto to examine the images at length before he carried on with his explanation.

'So Doctor Zuriaga waited for the right circumstances to get his revenge. Of course, he wanted to leave no trace, but he needed to get on to an island with restricted access and a sentry box guarded twenty-four hours a day, and he needed to get away unseen. But, you see, Zuriaga had been to Toralla a couple of times and knew that, when it rained, the guards waved familiar cars through without leaving the comfort of the sentry box. So the first rainy night was the perfect opportunity. The doctor arranged to meet Reigosa somewhere, and they drove across the bridge together in the saxophonist's car. As Zuriaga had predicted, the security guard didn't come out. He just raised the barrier for the car to move on, and didn't notice that there was someone in the passenger seat. The darkness, the rain and the time of year, when the Toralla tower was empty of holidaymakers, made it very hard for anyone to see him that night.'

Caldas interrupted his hypothetical story to make sure Soto was following. Soto simply waved his hand, motioning him to go on.

'Once they were in the flat they had a couple of drinks like any other day. The doctor's attitude, his killer instinct, which had served him so well in business meetings, didn't arouse Reigosa's suspicions. Feigning passion, the doctor tied Reigosa's hands to the headboard of the bed. Reigosa was now at his mercy, and he discovered what was really going on too late. Zuriaga had coldly planned the most painful vengeance he was capable of imagining. Being a surgeon, he knew the devastating effect formaldehyde would have when injected into live tissue. After he heard Reigosa's terrified confession of blackmail, he gagged him to stop him shouting. Then he injected formaldehyde into Reigosa's defenceless penis, thus perpetrating his fatal revenge. You've seen the gruesome result of that injection in the autopsy room.'

Superintendent Soto nodded gently.

'As if one could forget it,' said Rafael Estévez, who had a very clear recollection of the saxophonist's genitals.

'Well, with all this you can certainly prove that Zuriaga knew Reigosa,' said the superintendent, holding up one of the pictures. 'We'd even have a clear indication that he was being blackmailed. But we're treading on thin ice here. To press charges against the doctor we'd need more than these conjectures. We'd need evidence.'

'We can get some,' said Caldas, going back to his story of the events on Toralla Island. 'While his lover lay dying the doctor did a great job of cleaning the flat. Any trace of his presence there, whether that night or another, could have been enough to link him to the crime in future and ruin his plan. He must have left the glasses on the living room table for the end, as he would have wanted to wipe the fingerprints off them. But something must have worked against his cold blood and made him flee in a rush. It may have been a light, a noise, I don't know, but the fact is that he left the building without wiping off those fingerprints. And although the cleaning woman ruined most of them, we were able to recover part of a fingerprint, which we can compare with the doctor's. If they match, we will have placed Dimas Zuriaga at the scene of the crime.'

'I still don't see enough evidence to charge a man like Zuriaga with murder,' replied the superintendent. 'Even if, for argument's sake, the print turns out to be his, it would only prove that Zuriaga has been at the musician's home. As for the way he contradicted himself, that can be easily explained away in terms of his fear of seeing the pictures come to light. Why don't you wait for the full report from forensics?'

'There's also the DJ,' said Caldas, who could not contemplate a retreat once he had started charging.

'Who?' asked Soto.

'As I've already told you, I think Zuriaga found there were two people blackmailing him. One was Reigosa. But it was his accomplice who took the pictures and sent out emails and instructions to the doctor.'

'Have you found him?' asked Soto with interest, expecting more solid evidence than he had heard so far.

Leo confirmed they had.

'Last night. He worked as a DJ in a gay bar on Arenal Street called the Idílico.'

'I see,' said Soto, giving Estévez a reproachful look as he remembered the lawsuit which, thanks to his behaviour, that team of gay lawyers was filing against the police force.

'The boy said he knew Reigosa,' said Caldas. 'He told me Reigosa wasn't a regular, but went to the Idílico now and then. However, he seemed a bit evasive when I asked him about a man with extremely white hair – the doctor's most salient physical trait, as you've no doubt noticed.'

The superintendent confirmed he had with a slight nod.

'When I told him Reigosa had been killed,' continued Caldas, 'the boy looked like he was scared of something. I got the impression that he didn't feel safe there, and he refused to talk any further in the bar. We arranged to meet today at five in the afternoon, at a place far enough from where he lived, from the station and from his work.'

'And what did you get?' asked Soto.

'Nothing, sir. The DJ didn't make it to our appointment,' explained Caldas. 'His name was Orestes Grial. He's the boy who's turned up with a shot in the back of the neck at a flat on Camelias Road. I'm convinced it was Zuriaga who did him in.'

The superintendent, who'd known for a couple of hours about the new crime in the city, passed a hand over his face.

'Is that another hypothesis, Leo?'

'For the moment it is, sir. But the photographs you have on your desk were stored on the dead man's computer. I bet Orestes's death happened a little after one, when we left Zuriaga's mansion. The doctor must have gone to the boy's house. Orestes worked until seven in the morning, so he must have been sleeping at the time. Orestes seemed quite frightened when I spoke to him. The doctor must have threatened to go to the police if he didn't open the door. Once inside, he only had to wait for the boy to lower his guard and shoot him. Incidentally, Zuriaga doesn't remember leaving his house. He claims he's been at home for days, sunk in depression. His wife, however, casually said that the doctor went out on some errands in the afternoon. It seems our visits have healing powers.'

Soto raised a hand and Caldas stopped his exposition.

'Leo, all this doesn't quite fit together. How could Zuriaga have known that you'd been to see Orestes Grial the night before when you hadn't even paid Zuriaga himself a visit?'

'He didn't. But in the morning I'd told him that I had a witness who was prepared to confirm he knew Reigosa. In fact I was only trying to make him nervous, to confuse him and see if I could trip him up,' explained Caldas. 'Zuriaga must have come to his own conclusions and decided to kill off the other blackmailer before the boy could talk. Then he pulled the necessary strings to make sure we didn't come near him.'

'They must have got tangled,' replied Soto in a whisper.

Estévez smiled, and relaxed a bit now his superior's conjectures were seen to be more than mere flights of fancy.

'A few minutes ago they informed me that a glove's turned up. I guess you know of it, sir?'

'Yes, I've got the note here somewhere.' Soto found the paper in a drawer. 'They've found a latex glove in the rubbish bin nearest to the hall of Orestes's house,' he said, skimming the text. 'Apparently, it has traces of powder on it.'

'If I'm right, sir, we should find Zuriaga's DNA on the inside.'

'In that case, the doctor would be in hot water,' said Soto, who was starting to give in to Caldas's theory.

'The pieces will all fit together as soon as Isidro Freire appears.'

'Who?' asked the superintendent, who wasn't familiar with that name.

'A guy with a little black dog,' put in Estévez, earning himself a reproachful look from Caldas.

'Isidro Freire works at Riofarma. He's the sales representative in charge of the Vigo area,' explained Caldas to his superior. 'He's the one who provides the Zuriaga Foundation with formaldehyde. If you ask my opinion, I don't think Freire will turn up alive either.'

'Oh, come on, Leo!' exclaimed the superintendent, but Caldas ignored the comment and carried on.

'Isidro Freire is the link between Zuriaga and the formaldehyde, between the murderer and the weapon. I've asked for a list of the salesman's telephone calls, and over the last few days he called Zuriaga's home number several times. Freire has not shown up at the office today, and he's not answering the phone either. You know what, sir? If Zuriaga got rid of Luis Reigosa and then of Orestes Grial, I see no reason to believe that he may have spared Freire's life – that is, if Freire was indeed able to implicate him in the murder of the musician.'

The superintendent remained silent before Caldas's line of reasoning. The inspector stood up.

'Now you know what Zuriaga's doing here, sir.'

Rain

It rained on 20 May. It felt like winter.

At one thirty in the afternoon, Leo Caldas leaned on the bar and asked for some wine as an aperitif while he waited for the *luras* Carlos had found that morning in the market. Carlos had called him and other regulars to tell them of his extraordinary discovery, and to announce he would stew them for lunch in the traditional way, in a light wine sauce with onions, laurel and potatoes. Attracted by the promise of the small cephalopods, Leo had arrived early at the tavern. The dons were also in front of their wine mugs at that unusual hour. All four of them, like Caldas, normally came to the Eligio in the evening, but they had been bewitched by the idea of the sea delicacy and had fitted it into their schedules.

As on every day in the last week, the front page of the local paper gave plenty of space to the 'Zuriaga affair'. The case had become a sort of popular lynching of the notable arts patron. Although the trial had yet to start, the press had already sentenced him. They accused him of being a brutal serial killer and a homosexual with depraved tastes.

The doctor still claimed he was innocent, in spite of the mounting evidence against him. His team of lawyers hung firmly to the fact that the fingerprint found on the glass in Reigosa's flat did not match the doctor's, which meant there was no proof Zuriaga had been at the flat on Toralla Island at the moment of the crime.

However, there wasn't much they could do about the results of the analysis of the latex glove. These confirmed both that the powder on the outside had come from a firearm such as had been used to kill Orestes, and that there were traces of Zuriaga's DNA on the inside.

The lead picture in the paper showed an exhausted Zuriaga, flanked by one of his lawyers and his niece Diana. The doctor, visibly disheartened, seemed about to concede defeat at any moment. But, in spite of all the difficulties, his niece fought without rest to establish his innocence. As the present spokesperson of his uncle, Diana Alonso Zuriaga took every opportunity the press gave her to publicly call attention to the doctor's outstanding altruistic career, and to strongly condemn the injustice to which, in her view, he was being subjected.

The doctor's wife had not shown her face in public. The papers reported she had stayed at the family home ever since her husband had been arrested and was sunk in a severe depression.

↩

'These people are in big trouble,' said Carlos, pointing at the paper as he filled Caldas's mug with wine.

'They are.'

From a nearby table, a don who was flicking through the paper asked Caldas if he'd been involved in the Zuriaga case.

'I had something to do with it,' he replied tersely.

'They should write a novel about your adventures, Leo,' said another of the professors.

'Of course,' agreed the inspector with a wink.

'I mean it,' insisted the don, 'crime novels do very well.'

'Well, go ahead,' said Caldas, taking a sip from his mug.

Caldas mulled over the professors words as he savoured the pleasantly sour aftertaste of the wine.

Suddenly, like a bursting bubble, that nagging feeling he'd had for so many days stopped. And as it did, it brought back a vivid memory, allowing him to identify that which had attracted his attention on his first inspection of Reigosa's flat but had failed to stay in his mind.

He remembered the dead man's bookshelves with great clarity, and they had been full of crime novels. He remembered too that one of the books on the night table belonged to that genre. However, the other one, which had a bookmark in it, was something completely different, a nearly eight-hundred-page volume by Hegel.

Although it wasn't relevant at all for the case, he was relieved.

'Do you think it's normal for a man who usually reads crime novels to read Hegel's *Lessons in the Philosophy of History* before going to sleep?' he asked in the direction of the professors.

A bit surprised, all eyes turned to the oldest of the four.

'Well, I don't know,' he said, as if the others' gazes forced him to speak. 'I'd say that, in spite of the metaphors he uses to clarify his theories, Hegel is too rich a meal to digest at bedtime.'

His three learned dining companions agreed.

'Wasn't it Hegel who wrote one of the most notorious defences of the Inquisition?' put in Carlos from behind the bar, showing his background as an experienced manager of the illustrated tavern.

'You could see it that way, Carlos, though only up to a point. Hegel tends to justify anything that brings mankind closer to salvation – the salvation of the soul, that is. And in that sense you could say he might justify any Torquemada,' explained the old professor, 'for Hegel welcomes pain if it's a cause for repentance.'

Caldas found those words familiar. He remembered a caller had said something of the like on his radio show, and it seemed a strange coincidence. He picked up his mobile phone, dialled the radio's number, and asked to be put through to production.

'I'm sorry to trouble you, Rebeca.'

'Leo, what a surprise! Is anything wrong?'

'No, I only wanted to ask you whether it would be possible to trace a call we received on the programme. Just out of curiosity.'

'If it's recent, there's no problem. Programmes are recorded and kept on file for a while. What date are you after?'

'It was last week, but I can't remember the exact day,' said Caldas hesitantly. 'I'm sure you remember it better than me. I'm trying to trace that caller who didn't let Losada utter a word. A guy who said just one sentence, a bit of an apocalyptic phrase, and then hung up.'

'I know who you mean. The boss went into a bit of a tizzy after that call,' replied Rebeca. 'I'm sure I have it to hand. We keep a record of abusive callers, pranksters and crazy guys like this one. That way, if they call again, we don't put them through. It's not a very reliable filter, but it's better than nothing,' she explained. 'Now let's see ... Yes, here it is. He was called Angel, although I doubt that was his real name. The phrase he said was "Let us welcome pain if it is cause for repentance". He said it twice, quite slowly, and I managed to write it down. Hopefully we'll recognise him if he ever calls again.'

'Thanks, Rebeca, you're a marvel,' he said, pleased at how quickly the producer had found the sentence. It seemed a bit odd that the caller should have quoted from the very same book that was on Reigosa's night table.

'Do you want to write down the number, Leo?'

That was more than he'd expected.

'Go on,' he said, borrowing a ballpoint pen sticking out of the pocket of Carlos's shirt.

'Anything else?' she kindly asked after dictating it.

'Actually, yes. Is it possible to find out what day the call was made?'

'Of course, Leo. It was 12 May.'

Caldas double-checked the date of Luis Reigosa's murder. There it was: he'd been killed on the night of 11 May.

After he rang off he experienced that strange feeling that coincidences give rise to. He was about to ring the number that Rebeca had just given him when he thought better of it, and instead decided to ring up the police station and obtain an address.

'This is Caldas, I need an address for this number, please.'

As he waited, he listened to the professors. Mugs in hand, they were still considering various approximations to Hegel. They had reached the democratic, if simplistic, conclusion, that the German philosopher's had been an insufferable bore above all.

'Inspector?' the voice on the other end of the line said. 'That's not a private number. It's a public phone in a hospital.'

'Which one?' asked Caldas with the sense of unease of someone who thinks he already knows the answer.

'The Zuriaga Foundation, inspector,' said the officer, thus confirming Caldas's hunch.

'Many thanks,' muttered Caldas and rang off.

He slumped on to a bench by one of the windows in the tavern, and stared fixedly at the raindrops splattering against the glass framed in green wood. He didn't even move when he smelled the steaming stew that Carlos was bringing to the table.

'God save the *luras*!'

The inspector went out into the street.

No one paid attention to him.

Twist

Inspector Caldas walked down between the rows of desks at the police station. As he went past Estévez, he motioned him to follow. He went through the glass door of his office, hung his jacket on the coat rack, slumped into his black leather chair and picked up the phone.

'What's the matter, chief?' asked Estévez.

'I'd like you to do me a favour,' replied the inspector cupping the receiver. 'Call Riofarma, speak to Ramón Ríos, and find out if there's any news on Isidro Freire.'

Estévez left the office and disappeared among the desks.

'Forensics? Inspector Caldas here. May I speak to Clara Barcia?'

Since he'd left Eligio's, the inspector wanted a word with the officer who had led the inspection of Reigosa's flat. He knew how meticulous Clara's work was and trusted she would be of help.

'Clara, it's Caldas,' he said when she came on. 'I'd like to ask you a question about the Reigosa case, at the Toralla tower. Do you remember the book on the night table?'

'Hegel's or the other one?' asked the officer.

'Hegel's. Did you notice anything odd about it? A mark of some kind, a note, a dedication, a label, anything?'

'Except for an underlined sentence I didn't see anything out of the ordinary, inspector.'

'What underlined sentence?'

'There was a sentence underlined in pencil, inspector. It was on the same page as the bookmark.'

'Do you remember what it said?' asked Caldas.

'The sentence? I can't remember verbatim, but it was a bit

morbid, something about accepting pain and repenting,' replied Clara.

'Are you sure?' asked Caldas tensely.

'More or less, yes,' she said hesitantly.

'Why haven't I been informed of this?'

'It's all in the report, inspector,' answered Clara in a reedy voice.

'In the report?'

Caldas had not read Clara Barcia's final report. After Dimas Zuriaga's arrest, he had considered the case closed and had not looked back. His job was finished once a suspect had been captured and the evidence had been put forward; then the court of first instance took over.

'I added a handwritten note to the effect that the sentence seemed to confirm your theory of a crime of passion,' said Clara. Her voice betrayed a measure of surprise at the tone Caldas was employing with her. 'Did you not read it?'

Caldas didn't answer. He limited himself to shifting a pile of papers lying on his desk.

'As the doctor had already been arrested,' the officer went on, 'I didn't think it was necessary to bring your attention to it.'

The inspector turned over a stapled dossier which was hidden under a stack of other documents. It was Clara Barcia's report, with all her conclusions concerning the murder.

'Shit,' muttered Caldas. 'I'm sorry, Clara, I'll talk to you later.'

He hung up and quickly flicked through the pages, searching for the transcription of the sentence. He was pretty sure it hadn't been underlined just by chance. And he confirmed it when he read it: 'Let us welcome pain if it is cause for repentance'.

'Shit, shit,' he repeated as he read it over and over.

'May I come in, chief?' interrupted Rafael Estévez.

'Any news on Freire?' asked Caldas without lifting his eyes from the dossier.

Estévez shook his head.

'He hasn't turned up at the office since the day of our visit.'

The inspector put down the report, steepled his hands and rested his mouth on them.

'Of course he hasn't,' he mumbled. 'What an idiot I've been.'

Caldas stood up, got his jacket and quickly walked out of his office, with his assistant trying hard to keep up.

~

The two policemen were driving along the waterfront. It was raining hard, and they couldn't see the road clearly. Although it was only mid-afternoon, the sky was as dark as the sea.

'What do you mean it wasn't him?' asked a disorientated Estévez. 'But it was you who put all the evidence together to arrest him.'

'All I'm saying for now is that it might not have been him. There's that possibility,' replied Caldas from the passenger seat.

Estévez didn't understand his sudden change of mind.

'Would you mind telling me what's happened to make you think he might be innocent?'

'You can have smoke without a fire,' replied Caldas cryptically.

'I'm sorry, inspector, but I haven't got my Rosetta Stone with me. Are you going to tell me or are we playing charades again?'

Caldas didn't know exactly what he was looking for. He'd been wrong once before and didn't intend to be wrong once again. In addition, he knew that thoughts, like wine, needed time to settle. Yet he decided to tell Estévez what was going through his mind.

'The day Reigosa turned up dead I got a call at the radio. A man said the phrase: "Let us welcome pain if it is cause for repentance". It's a quote from Hegel, which the caller repeated twice, for us to hear it clearly. Every week we get weird calls,' explained the inspector, 'so that call wouldn't have been important at all if there had not been, on Reigosa's night table, a book by that very same German thinker, Hegel. That book didn't fit in with the other books Reigosa had at home, which were a lot lighter. And somehow I can't imagine Reigosa curling up with a volume of nineteenth-century philosophy after a concert.'

'I don't see why not,' replied Estévez. 'If he didn't mind sleeping with men, I don't see what's wrong with Hegel, to be honest.'

Caldas was too worried to laugh at the joke, and went on expounding his later discoveries, even though he hadn't intended to open his mouth for the rest of the journey. He realised that thinking out loud helped him select those facts that were really relevant.

'The volume had a bookmark in it, and on that page someone had underlined a phrase in pencil. I've just found out that it was the same phrase that the caller had uttered on air during my show.' Caldas interrupted the explanation for a moment to get a cigarette. 'All incoming calls at the radio station are recorded for a while,' he went on after he lit up. 'And that particular one had been made from a phone booth in the hall of the Zuriaga Foundation.'

'And what's so weird about that?' interrupted Estévez. 'I think it explains the case even better. Hegel's phrase confirms what we knew already – that the doctor wanted to inflict a gruesome punishment on the saxophonist as an act of revenge for his betrayal.'

'There I don't agree, Rafa. No one who's planning to murder someone sows clues all over the place in such a childish way. It all seems too neat, too deliberate,' said the inspector, winding down the window just a crack to let the smoke out. 'It can't be that easy.'

'Your intuition again, chief. Where I'm from we say that if it looks like a duck, it walks like a duck and it goes "quack", then it is a duck.'

'It's not my intuition, can't you see?'

For a few seconds, the only sound was the patter of the rain on the roof of the car and the screeching swing of the windscreen wipers.

'What is it I've got to see?' asked Estévez, who was unable to put his finger on what Caldas found so obvious.

'We followed the lead of the formaldehyde and we came to Dimas Zuriaga in two days,' explained the inspector. 'Everything happened too quickly – there wasn't enough time for the evidence to mature.'

'Is that wrong, chief? You should be proud at how quickly we found the murderer. Remember there were two victims. Three, if Freire turns up.'

'But it would have been more normal for us to get side-tracked until Clara found the phrase in the book.' This hypothesis was taking shape in the inspector's mind. 'And then I would have remembered that those were the same words someone had uttered on the radio show. Do you realise now?' he asked, looking fixedly at Estévez. Estévez nodded slightly, almost out of duty, and Caldas resumed his speculations.

'The call had been made from the Zuriaga Foundation, and so we would've concentrated our investigation there. With a little time and effort we would've found out about Zuriaga and Reigosa's relationship, because we know from experience that facts cannot remain hidden forever. Sooner or later we would have come to the doctor.'

'But that line of reasoning, far from exculpating Zuriaga, would incriminate him even more,' replied Estévez.

'You don't get it, Rafa. If the doctor is the murderer as you say, how do you explain that call to the radio station? And how would you account for his leaving the book with that same underlined phrase at Reigosa's? He might as well have left us a calling card.'

By now Caldas was sure that Hegel's book did not belong to Reigosa, but had been planted in the bedroom by the murderer, in order to incriminate someone else.

'There is a possibility, though, that the doctor may have wanted to play cat and mouse with you, inspector. Even if you don't admit it, you're someone in this city, same as he is. He may have left clues to test you. He wouldn't be the first one to do such a thing.'

'Have you seen Zuriaga's latest pictures in the papers?' asked Caldas. 'He looks completely washed out. Do you think a criminal who likes arm-wrestling with justice looks like that?'

Estévez didn't reply; he was aware of Zuriaga's deterioration.

'He's resigned to his fate, he's lowered his arms,' added Caldas. 'Hardly the attitude of someone fighting an intellectual battle.'

'There you're right,' conceded Estévez.

'Now, to return to the book and the call – killers take care to cover up their traces, not to leave any evidence lying around. Whoever planned this mess wanted all clues to point in one direction only, in the direction of Dimas Zuriaga,' concluded Caldas. 'I've got a feeling it's all a set-up. By chance I didn't fall for it, but, for unknown reasons, I've ended up exactly where the murderer wanted me to go in the first place – arresting the doctor and accusing him of murder.'

Estévez was not entirely convinced.

'Are you sure that we're on the right track now, chief?'

This far in the game, Caldas was no longer concerned about tracks; he simply wanted to arrive at the truth. Only a few hours before, he had no doubts that Zuriaga was guilty; now he was considering the possibility that he might be completely innocent. He had taken the wrong turn at some point during the investigation, but he was prepared to go back to square one and proceed in a different direction.

'I don't know if we are,' replied the inspector. 'I'm hoping to find Freire, and for him to clarify a couple of things.'

Estévez turned towards his superior.

'Do you think Freire is alive?' he asked, as he remembered that a short time ago his boss had assumed that the owner of the little black dog that had bitten his shoes at Riofarma was dead.

'Orestes was killed in a hurry. They didn't have time to prepare the crime. It's been eight days since Freire's disappearance, too many for a murdered corpse to remain hidden. I'm inclined to think that it's Freire himself who has no intention of coming out into the open,' said the inspector, his eyes fixed on the road, which was barely visible behind the curtain of rain. 'Besides, we've got all those calls to Zuriaga's house the days before the murder of Reigosa. Why would Freire need to speak to the doctor so often? Zuriaga had access to formaldehyde without the need to contact the distributor – he just needed to get it from his hospital. I don't know what he was after, but Freire was not trying to sell a few litres of formaldehyde to the doctor. It was something else.'

'Have they asked Zuriaga about Freire again?'

'Zuriaga keeps repeating the same – he doesn't know a thing about the crimes, doesn't know Freire, didn't know who Orestes was, and loved Reigosa deeply,' enumerated Caldas. 'He has not altered his declaration one iota in all these days.'

'And what do you have to say about the latex glove?' asked Estévez, who, although he had admired his boss's reasoning, still harboured doubts. 'Do you think Zuriaga didn't kill the DJ either?'

Caldas, who had no answer for that, limited himself to a shrug. He knew that the DNA was incontrovertible proof of Orestes Grial's murder: no judge would absolve Zuriaga of that. However, he still thought the glove didn't solve the puzzle of Reigosa's death and Freire's disappearance. The doctor's only hope might be hidden in some tiny detail that he, Caldas, had overlooked. The most difficult cases were often solved after a seemingly insignificant point was brought to attention.

Dimas Zuriaga was too shocked to remember, but Caldas trusted that someone near him might have noticed something, however small, that might help to establish his innocence.

Estévez stopped the car before the enormous wooden gate. Caldas raised his collar, got out of the car and, dodging puddles, walked over to the wall and rang the bell.

Under the heavy rain, the inspector waited for an answer.

Gap

The smell of wood panelling suffused the dark living room.

'You've got to make an effort, madam,' insisted Caldas, asking her to cast her mind back.

'You can't come here, after ruining my life, and ask me to make an effort,' replied the woman, running her words together. 'How can you be so heartless? My husband is in jail because of you, he's going to be judged for such gruesome crimes I don't even want to think about them, and you've got the gall to come here and rub it in my face over and over again?'

'There might be a chance your husband isn't guilty of all the crimes he's being accused of.'

'Of course he's not, inspector, he's not guilty at all,' moaned Mercedes Zuriaga, slumping on to a sofa and bursting into tears.

The policemen stood there, in respectful silence, waiting for her to calm down. They felt awkward confronted with Mrs Zuriaga's transformation; there was no trace of the elegant woman who had received them so gracefully but a few days before. The house, as if in sympathy, had also gone from constant activity to sombre stillness, from light to darkness.

'Mrs Zuriaga.' It was Estévez turn now: 'Try to remember if Isidro Freire visited your husband. We're sure they spoke on the phone regularly in the days after the murder. It could be important for your husband.'

'I've already told you I know no Isidro Freire,' she said, as she wiped the tears away from her puffy eyes. 'I've never monitored Dimas's calls. I'm not his secretary. I'm Doctor Zuriaga's wife!' she added with a flash of dignity.

Estévez nodded. Seeing Zuriaga's wife in such a state was too much for him. As for Caldas, he knew that opening these wounds would prove very painful, but he wanted no gaps in his inquiry.

'You must have seen or heard something. Freire sold medical supplies. He phoned your husband several times in the days before our first visit.' The inspector pressed the point. 'They must have discussed products, probably formaldehyde. Didn't you hear anything?'

The woman shook her head.

'Maybe he was here under a different name,' added Caldas, trying another approach so as to jog the woman's memory. In his haste he may have condemned Dimas Zuriaga to a personal hell, but Caldas still wanted to leave the house with some kind of hope for him. '*Someone* must have visited in the last couple of weeks.'

'Yes, you two. You burst into our house and shattered my husband's life and mine,' she paused to take a breath. 'You've destroyed a family. Do you know what that is? Have you any idea what the word *family* means?' The woman was once again moaning bitterly, burying her face in her long hands. 'You're scum.'

Rafael Estévez offered her a handkerchief as he implored Caldas with his eyes to leave the woman alone. Caldas gave up and placed his card on one of the low tables in that huge living room.

'It's OK, Mrs Zuriaga. We're going back to the station now. I'll leave my card here. Should you remember anything, do not hesitate to call me.'

'I'll walk you to the door,' said Mercedes Zuriaga, wiping her tears with Estévez's handkerchief.

'There's no need, madam,' said the officer.

She ignored this reply, stood up and led them down the hallway to the imposing front door.

'Goodbye, inspector,' she muttered, offering her hand. 'I hope I never see you again.'

Mercedes Zuriaga opened the door, and a small dog with curly black fur slipped in.

'Pipo! Get out of the house right now!' she shouted.

Officer Estévez, his eyes on stalks, stared at Freire's little dog, which was once again having a go at his shoelaces.

Caldas turned to the doctor's wife.

'Where is Isidro Freire, madam?'

'I don't know what you're talking about,' replied the woman, holding the door to let them out. 'Now, if you please...'

'Where?' asked Caldas again, without budging.

'Don't you have any respect for *anything*?' she reproached him, once again bursting into tears. 'I've already told you I don't know who that man is, inspector.'

Leo Caldas was not buying it.

'You know perfectly well, madam – Isidro Freire is the sales representative from Riofarma, and the owner of that dog,' he said, pointing to Pipo.

'That's not possible,' she mumbled through her sobs.

'Enough of this farce!' ordered Caldas. 'The doctor may not be an ideal husband, but he's not a murderer,' he said, getting closer to her. 'I think you should come with us to the station, you've got a lot to explain.'

Mercedes Zuriaga stopped sobbing, and Caldas saw her fix him with eyes that had suddenly turned as cold as ice.

When, on the way to the car, he asked again about Isidro Freire's whereabouts, the woman gestured in the direction of the sea.

'He's down there on the boat, terrified.'

Caldas asked Estévez to go and fetch him, and Mercedes Zuriaga added with disdain:

'Another coward, just like Dimas. They're all cowards.'

Motive

In the course of the interrogation, Mercedes Zuriaga related how, shortly after she and Zuriaga had started courting, she left her job as a nurse to become the famous doctor's wife, and found herself living in greater splendour than she had ever thought possible.

However, in spite of a good start, the long days Zuriaga spent at the Foundation ended up killing their passion, and soon enough their marriage was reduced to little more than the amicable relationship of two people who simply lived together. Mercedes resigned herself to Dimas's absences and lack of affection. Even if she had an unfulfilled love life, she still held her husband in deep admiration.

She related how, over their two decades together, she had always respected the fact that the doctor preferred intellectual to physical pleasure. But she started being suspicious when, three years ago, she noticed that he had started taking greater care of his appearance and that, without her even asking, he would make excuses when he came home late from work. Mercedes thought he might be seeing another woman, and decided to find out if there were grounds for her suspicions. She was amazed to discover, however, that the reason for those excuses was a man: Luis Reigosa, a saxophonist who lived on Toralla Island.

She felt threatened for months, until she realised Dimas was not planning to leave her. She decided to carry on as if nothing had happened: in a way, she had lost her husband a long time before. But she did promise herself she would not be cast aside after so many years of sacrifices.

Once the initial shock had passed, Mercedes started sailing more often, and in this way she met Isidro Freire, a handsome young man who shared her hobby and who, by becoming her lover, had a soothing effect on her frustrations. She even pulled some strings to get him a job at Riofarma, a laboratory near her husband's hospital.

Time went by until, a few weeks previously, she'd found a compromising email on her husband's laptop, complete with pictures. Upon reading it she realised there was a chance her husband might be forced to make a choice and abandon her for Reigosa.

Ever since she had learned of her husband's relationship with the musician, she wondered how she might be able to make it end if she needed to. And she had convinced herself that the best solution would be to eliminate Reigosa and leave circumstantial evidence pointing to Dimas. The murder should look both like a crime of passion and the work of a doctor. One afternoon, lying with her lover on the deck of her boat, she found the perfect method while flicking through Riofarma's catalogue, and noticing the safety guidelines indicated on one of the products.

Coldly, she explained that her first move had been to follow her husband on one of the days he made a payment to his blackmailer. By then she had decided not to let the extortion ruin her plans. She saw Dimas leave a bag containing the money behind some shrubs, and she hid until a young man, who was none other than Orestes Grial, appeared for the pick-up. She approached him and informed him she knew all about the extortion and could report him to the police at any moment. The man was terrified, and he swore he'd never send the doctor another message in exchange for Mercedes Zuriaga's silence. He also promised to let her know if anyone ever declared an interest in the doctor or his lover in his presence.

Mercedes went back home and, enticing Freire with the promise of sharing the doctor's great personal wealth, convinced him to seduce the saxophonist. They decided to do it on a rainy night, and they had a lucky strike on the first night they tried. She knew Reigosa sometimes sought brief encounters with other men, who found his water-blue eyes irresistible. Reigosa was indeed in the mood for company on the night they chose, and Isidro Freire was at the Idílico, ready to be noticed, and later to be taken to the flat on Toralla Island.

Once in the bedroom, as if in a fit of passion, Freire tied the musician to the headboard, gagged him, and went down to open the door for Mercedes, who had reached the island on her boat.

She came into the bedroom with gloved hands and injected formaldehyde into the musician's penis, while Freire fought to keep his legs still. After that, following a meticulously premeditated plan, Mercedes left Hegel's book, with its sentence about pain and repentance faintly underlined, on the bedside table next to the dying man. He writhed in pain as the formaldehyde spread throughout his body.

Isidro Freire, fighting back nausea, cleaned any traces of their presence from the bedroom. His accomplice took care of the living room on the upper floor, but she deliberately left the gin glasses from which Reigosa and Freire had drunk. That way, she insured herself against her lover in case he started to have doubts or decided to betray her, or if she simply wanted to change him for another. Once that was done, she sailed away from the island under cover of darkness. Freire drove out in Reigosa's car, which he abandoned in a forest after setting fire to it.

The following day, on one of his professional visits to the Zuriaga Foundation, Isidro Freire called Radio Vigo from one of the phones in the lobby of the hospital. When he was put through to the presenter of *Patrol on the Air*, he read Hegel's phrase twice, then hung up.

Once the police found the book, Zuriaga and Freire only needed to sit and wait for Leo Caldas, the famous patrolman, to remember that mysterious call to his show, tie up the loose ends, and link the crime to the Zuriaga Foundation –

and the doctor to the saxophonist. After that, with Reigosa gone and her husband not only behind bars but also repudiated by society, she'd be able to enjoy the fortune of the Zuriagas.

However, one afternoon Isidro Freire phoned her at home several times. He was frightened. Two police officers had been at the lab and questioned him about formaldehyde. The following morning, Orestes Grial, as good as his word, also informed her that two police officers were poking about to see if he knew anything about Reigosa and the doctor. He had managed to postpone a more formal talk until the following day.

The bloodhounds had failed to notice her bait and, even worse, were now tracking a more dangerous scent.

After those very same policemen visited her at home, Mercedes Zuriaga convinced herself she must silence Orestes Grial for good: she couldn't let the DJ compromise her. She turned up on his doorstep pretending she had money for him as a thank-you for his information.

The young man was sleeping when she knocked on his door; he got up to let her in and immediately excused himself. Mercedes Zuriaga grabbed a pillow to muffle the shot and followed the sleepy Orestes to the bathroom. She put on a latex glove and, on top of it, another one she had found, used, in the bin of her husband's office. Back in the street she disposed of the glove, leaving it where she thought the police would look for such a thing first.

The seed had been planted. Only water was needed now for the tree to grow and bear those fruits she was planning on enjoying.

'Pity about the dog,' said Caldas, remembering he wouldn't have found anything if it hadn't been for little Pipo.

'No, inspector,' corrected Mercedes Zuriaga, 'pity about men.'

In the Clear

Caldas walked under the heavy rain. It had gone eleven by the time Mercedes Zuriaga and Isidro Freire finished their confessions.

The inspector decided to visit the jazz bar in the old town for the third time in his life. He was in no mood for the solitude of his home. He needed to forget Dimas Zuriaga's bewildered face and clouded eyes as he had accepted his apologies.

Leo Caldas pushed open the door of the Grial, walked over to the bar and looked at the stage, where a group of musicians were about to begin the show. The small, fair-skinned woman greeted him with a nod. She then placed her pale hands on the keyboard, leaned forward a bit, and sang breathily into the microphone:

> *Some day he'll come along*
> *The man I love*
> *And he'll be big and strong*
> *The man I love*